Desperate Rescue

PAUL K. McAFEE

A Black Horse Western

ROBERT HALE · LONDON

ISBN 0 7090 7067 5

Robert Hale Limited
Clerkenwell House
Clerkenwell Green
London EC1R 0HT

Typeset by
Derek Doyle & Associates, Liverpool.
Printed and bound in Great Britain by
Antony Rowe Limited, Wiltshire

*This book is dedicated
with much love to my
wife, Shirley, and to
Mike, Tammi, Jennive,
Cindy and Trina*

ONE

Walt Harris paused in his splitting of a length of log into rails which would, along with hundreds of others like it, surround his pastures and his gardens. It was hard work, but he was used to hard work. He had come to this place when it was nothing but wilderness and with mainly strength and determination had built a cabin, unusual in those parts, for it had four rooms and a field-stone fire-place.

Here he had brought his wife and their two-year-old son. Now it had been six years, and the boy, Billy, was eight and able to take on many of the chores. He was a sturdy boy, with bright eyes and a ready smile. When he smiled, Walt saw his wife's face reflected in that of their son. Mary Harris was his right arm. She was by his side in all he did, approving, encouraging and delighted with what they had, together, done in making a home in the wilds of the Colorado canyon country.

Walt looked out over the pastures he had cleared. A small herd of a hundred cattle grazed there. He now owned six horses, some for work and another for riding. He wiped his face with a bandanna and felt a surge of pride in that which had been done. This was their

7

destiny. This was their land! Their labor, sweat and strain-
ing had gone into every moment of its creation.

Leaving Denver a month after arriving there, he had
followed a thin trail into the mountains. It lifted and
turned and twisted and then, all at once, opened upon
this small, cupped valley he now called home. Rimmed
by mountains on all sides, with a small creek running
through the center of it, he immediately saw its potential.
Within weeks, he was back erecting a temporary cabin,
widening a spring back of the house and preparing to
bring his family. Mary had fallen in love with the valley
the moment she saw it, and from that time on there was
no questions in either of their minds. This was theirs,
their home, their land!

Walt took up his broad-ax again and turned to making
rails for his pasture fence. Mary was working in the
garden and Billy was helping her. Life was what you made
of it, he thought as he plied the ax again, and this was
good.

Mary Harris was from pioneer stock. Her family came
into Indiana slightly after the Revolutionary War and,
homesteading, created a good life for the family, and a
farm that produced all that was needed for survival in
what was then a wilderness.

Mary was reared to expect to work hard for her livelihood. She gave little thought to the niceties for young
women and, with the exception of a community square-
dance occasionally, had little social contact with those of
her own age.

When Walt Harris came along she knew this was a man
for her life and when he proposed her 'yes' was fervent
and forthcoming. That now she was again on the edge of
a wilderness and working long hours to create a home
from the land, was accepted without question. This was

the way of life. When she found she was pregnant with Billy, she felt her life was fulfilled and found a deep satisfaction in all she and her husband and son were doing.

She raised her head from a patch of weeds she was hoeing as her son called to her.

'Mom. What do Indians look like?'

She smiled and wiped the sweat from her forehead. The agile mind of a boy. Now it was Indians.

'I'm told they are much like us, only darker. But don't worry. The Indians in this part of the country are not dangerous.'

'If you say so, Mom. But there's one standing down there across the creek looking up at the house!'

He was tall, slender and muscular. His long hair was pulled back and tied behind with a leather cord. His face was angular with the slightly curved center as seen in the mountain Indians. His eyes were black and glittering. He looked long and intently at the well-built cabin, the well-constructed sheds, the pastures of long grass for the animals and the garden, now being worked by the woman. He grunted softly. this was as it should be, the woman working. But the man was working hard, too. He should have another squaw to do the extra work. Then his thoughts focused. He should not be here. The white man was on Indian land, killing the game and using the riches of the earth for himself. His gaze hardened. He made a gesture and was joined by five other warriors. All were painted and carried bows. One carried a rifle, army issue, stolen from a dead American soldier. The leader wore no paint; from his forehead for several inches back and to the side, was a streak of white, almost silvery hair.

He was called Lightning Head, on account of the

blazed streak in his hair. He was the war chief of his tribe and was known far and wide for his many coups in battle.

The Indians mounted on small mountain ponies and, led by Lightning Head, they dashed across the creek and up the pasture slope towards the cabin.

'Here they come, Ma!' Billy ran from the shed where he had stood in the doorway watching the Indians. 'Run, Ma ... get Pa!'

Mary whirled and, seeing the charging Indians, threw down her hoe and raced toward the cabin. 'Get in the cabin, Billy!' she screamed.

Walt heard his wife scream and whirled round, dropping his ax and grabbing his shotgun that leant on a log beside him. He saw an Indian on a spotted pony racing toward him, whirling a tomahawk in preparation for striking him down with one blow. He leveled the shotgun and fired, the load catching the rider in the chest, tearing him screaming from the pony. There was a round left in the other barrel of the shotgun, but Walt got no chance to discharge it. A second Indian followed the first and, leaning from his pony, crashed headlong into the white man.

They rolled and the Indian leaped to his feet. Before Walt could rise the Indian leaped upon him with a gleaming knife, and slashed his throat with one savage thrust. Walt wilted, grabbing his throat, his hands covered with his spurting life's blood. He fell back, never seeing his wife felled by the tomahawk blow from another warrior.

During the few minutes of the fatal death of the two whites, man and woman, Lightning Head sat his horse at he edge of the cleared space about the cabin, watching the slaughter. He caught a movement by a quick glance towards one of the sheds, to see a tousled head disappear from the doorway. Walking the animal slowly, he approached the shed. Motioning to one of his men, he pointed to the shed and watched as the man entered. There was a scrambling, a yelling, and the warrior came out carrying a fighting Billy under his arm. The white boy was frightened, yet unwilling to submit. He kicked, slapped and hit with hard, small fists, until the Indian grew irritated and tossed him to the ground, seizing his knife from his belt. He drew back to slash the boy when Lightning Head spoke.

'No!' He gestured to Billy's captor. The Indian paused with the knife raised above Billy's face.

'He is old enough to fight, he is old enough to cause trouble,' the warrior said to his chief. 'Better he go the way of his parents.'

'No! I will take him. He will learn the way of the Ute and become a warrior with them.'

'A white warrior?' The Indian dropped Billy's arm. 'He is yours as chief. But he will be much trouble in the camp.'

'Put him on the horse before me,' Lightning Head ordered. 'I will teach him the ways of our people.' Growling, the man lifted Billy and flung him across the horse before the seated rider.

Billy straightened and then attempted to slide from the animal. Lightning Head tightened his grip on the boy. He shook him and then holding him tightly, spoke in hoarse, broken English.

'Boy not fight. See,' Lightning Head pointed to the body of Walt Harris. Father is dead. Mother is dead. You go with me. Be my boy to help squaw in village. Not be hurt.'

Billy saw the inert body of his father. He twisted in the Indian's arms and saw his mother lying between the garden and the back of the cabin. She did not move. He turned his face to the sky, stiffened and screamed a long, heart-rending scream, and then slumped in the arms of the Indian, drained and dulled by fright and by the horror of seeing his parents lying dead, he wilted in the arms of his captor.

Lightning Head made a gesture toward the cabin. 'Burn it,' he said. Two of his followers made torches of straw from the barn and in lighting them, tossed them into the barn, the shed and the house. When the group rode away from the Harris ranch, the buildings were aflame. None of them looked back. With Billy, still struggling, hanging across the pony with Lightning Head holding him tightly, they disappeared into the canyon back of the ranch and were gone.

TWO

Clarence Harris looked up from where he was wiping spilled beer from the bar of the Last Chance saloon as a huge man came through the bat-wing doors. He paused and a slow grin spread over his face.

'By all the gods, it's Charlie Webb! You rascal you, where have you been? We all decided the grizzlies had got you.' He dropped his rag on the bar and came around, approaching the visitor with outstretched hand.

His hand disappeared into the huge paw of the man and Charlie Webb's booming laugh rattled the bottles on the shelf back of the bar.

'Been holed up on the mountains, Clarence. I decided I had to come out and see civilization again before I went loco.'

'Well, belly up to the bar, old friend, and we'll get started on civilization with whatever you want – unless it's champagne. We're all out of it.'

Webb followed him, his large body moving gracefully. 'Don't mind if I do. A cool beer will do to start with.'

Charlie Webb was a man of the mountains. He had come into the Colorado country ten years before, while still a very young man. Teaming up with an experienced mountain man, he had shed his Eastern ways and now

13

would not consider returning to his Eastern roots. He was six feet six inches tall, with a weight that held steady at two hundred and twenty. He towered over most of those he met, yet he did not use his physical advantage in an obnoxious manner. He was good natured and his laugh was more frequent than his anger. He was liked by most men he met, and those that did not like him were not about to cause his anger to be directed at them.

Having lived in the Colorado mountains, and in particular in the canyon country, there was no doubt as to his courage. No man spent years hunting, trapping, trading with Indians, if he did not have the courage to face both the elements and the people he met. There were tales told of his strength and courage around camp-fires, and in the lodges of the red men. Charlie Webb was a *man* and recognized as such by white and red men alike.

Webb leaned against the bar and received the mug of beer Clarence handed him. He sipped and sighed and saluted his friend with it.

'This is the best-tasting drink I've had in years, Clarence. Get ready to pull another.'

'Did you bring in some plews?' Clarence poured himself a beer and joined his friend. There were only a few customers in the room as it was merely midday. The drinkers would begin to come in about four and by six o'clock he, and his helper, would be busy. Right now he had time to visit with an old friend he had not seen for at least three years.

'Beaver are getting scarce, as I think you know,' Webb replied. 'I found a little river back there that had not been touched, so I pruned it a little, taking out only the full grown and leaving the younger ones for seed. If no one else locates it, I'll have a source of plews for some time to come.'

'Good thinking,' Clarence told him. He eyed his friend closely. 'Are you in a hurry this morning? I've something I want to ask you.'

Webb shook his head. 'Nope. Gonna get my plews out of the livery where I left them and see what I can get for them.'

Clarence cocked his head, with a wry smile. 'Bill Weaver at the mercantile is buying hides. He'll give you a good price. Besides,' he grinned, 'I'm half-owner of Bill's store, so you'd be working with me, too.'

Webb laughed. 'I'll see what Bill has to offer. What did you want to talk about?'

The saloon-keeper went to the door of a back room and called to his helper. 'Take the bar for a little while, Randy. I've got some palavering to do with a friend.' He poured each another beer and gestured to a table at the back of the room. 'Come on back there. We can talk and Randy can take care of the customers, if there are any.'

Seated at the table, Clarence leaned across so his voice would not carry. 'Charlie, you knowed my nephew, Walt, didn't you?'

Webb nodded. 'I've met him here, after he got to Denver. Got him a small ranch up in the canyon country, didn't he?'

Clarence nodded. 'He found some high meadows up there with just the amount of ground he needed for a small cattle- and horse-ranch. He didn't expect nor try to be big. Just enough to raise some prize horses to sell to the army and enough beef for themselves and to ship now and then for workin' money.' He shook his head, his face suddenly full of lines of sorrow. 'A war party came by. At least that is the best we could figure out. Anyway, they kilt Walt an' his wife, Mary.' He fell silent.

Webb shook his head. 'That's bad, Clarence. And it's

unexpected hereabouts. There's been no Indian trouble
for four or five years. Were here any signs that give some
idea just who they were? What tribe they might have been
from?'

Clarence shrugged. 'Just an arrow or two here and
there. They burned the cabin and the sheds. Most of the
buildings burnt to the ground. But, that's not the worst
of it.' He paused.

'Charlie, they musta carried off Walt's son, Billy. We
searched everywheres. We stirred all the ashes of the
house and sheds, and there were no burned bodies or
bones. He was a smart kid. If he had hid, and wasn't
caught, then he'd have made his way into Denver and to
my house.'

'How far out is the ranch?' asked Webb.

Clarence thought a moment. 'I'd say, about thirty
miles into the canyon country, and ten up some pretty
high mesas. It's a two-day ride to get there, not pushing
your horse. Billy could have walked it out in three or four
days, easily.'

'Has the trail leading there and back been searched?'

'Yes, several times. I rode and walked it myself three or
for times, looking and yelling. It's high, where he was,
and some of them canyons echo for miles.'

Webb sighed. He slipped a well-used pipe from his
pocket, tamped it tightly with tobacco, lighted it and
smoked slowly and thoughtfully. 'It runs in my mind that
there is an Indian camp about fifty miles up the canyon
country, in a high valley among the mountains there. It's
the closest to Denver. Could be a hunting-party come
through and saw Walt's place. If they were a mind to,
they just might have done that killing and burning. Right
now, with pressure from the government to get as many
as possible on reservations, they might be of a mind to

get rid of any white eyes they came across.'

Clarence nodded. 'That's been my thinkin'.' He eyed Webb for a longer moment. 'Charlie, would you be of a mind to do a little scouting up that a-ways, an' see if there's a possibility they might be holdin' my nephew's boy? An' if you, being' a mountain man, might figure out a way to get him out of there, we'd be mightily grateful. An',' he hastened to add, 'we'd make it worth your efforts.'

Webb was silent a long spell, smoking his pipe and sipping on his beer. Finally he stirred his shoulders. 'Clarence, let me think on it tonight. I'll give you my answer in the morning. Right now, I aim to get my plews out of the livery over to the mercantile and then find a barbershop and a bathtub.'

Clarence nodded and rose. 'Come on in after breakfast tomorrow an' we'll talk about it some more.' He paused and then continued, 'I don't reckon there's another man hereabout that might be able to find and rescue the boy.'

Charlie Webb left the saloon and walked up the street toward the livery where he had left his pack mule and a load of prime beaver-pelts. Selected carefully over several months, they were of best quality and should bring top price.

He retrieved his huge bundle of skins from the office of the liveryman, shouldered it and stepped through the large doors onto the street. Three men faced him.

'Wa'al, lookee here,' one of them drawled. 'This ranny has latched onto our plews. What do you think, fellers?'

One nodded, his eyes glinting as he saw the size of the bundle. 'He sure has, Lafe.'

The liveryman, an oldster crippled by a wild bronc he

was once attempting to tame, limped out of the door behind Webb.

'You men are wrong. This man brought them plews in this morning an' left them here with me until he could find a buyer—'

'You keep your nose outta this, old man!' The third man, a skinny, mean-faced individual, wore a sixgun strapped low on his right thigh. 'Just get back into your stable an' ferget about this. These plews are ourn.' He glared at the liveryman and the old man stared back, then shrugged and stepped back into the barn.

Webb had been eyeing the men and knew them for what they were; thieves, roughnecks of the town, and given to bluster and bullying to get their way. He shook his head.

'You boys are wrong. Wrong in two ways. Wrong in saying these hides are yours. Wrong to try taking them from me.'

The man Lafe spoke up, jeering. 'Oh, you're a big one, all right. But I reckon three of us can whittle you down to size. How about it boys? He's takin' our plews. Are we goin' to let him get away with it?'

'Naw. What's ourn is ourn. Let's take him!' One of the men spat and slapped his hands together with a loud 'pop'. 'Right now!'

The spokesman, Lafe, nodded and the three men moved in on Webb, one on each side and Lafe in the middle.

They were surprised when the big man, instead of retreating from them, stepped toward them, so that when they arrived close enough to launch their attack, he was there before them. Lafe grinned and drawing back, threw a roundhouse right at Webb's head. Webb dodged and seizing Lafe with huge hands, lifted him and whirling, threw him against the man nearest him. Both went down in a yelling sprawl. Lafe bounded up and was met with a fist to his temple and one to his belly, slamming him against the livery wall. He wilted and slid down, only half aware of any further confrontation with Webb.

The second man scrambled to his feet and, cursing, dived at Webb's legs. Webb sidestepped and as the man landed on the hard-packed ground in front of the livery, he reached down and, seizing the man, whirled him above his head and threw him against the wall to land beside Lafe, groaning with pain brought on by his crashing into the building.

The third man paused, seeing his companions suddenly taken from the fray. He stepped back and slapped his hand to the gun-butt on his right thigh. Webb's big hand darted in and slapped the weapon from the man's hand as it cleared leather. The sixgun landed yards away from its owner and he stepped back, pausing to run. But he was too late.

'Now, let's see what we can do to persuade you that those plews are mine,' Webb mused. Seizing the man, dodging his flailing arms, Webb lifted the man and carried him toward the door-frame of the livery.

'Do you mind if I hang some baggage I found on the street on the side of your establishment? Just until someone else comes and takes it away?' he asked the elderly liveryman who had come to the door as the fracas ended.

The old man shook his head. 'Nope, just as long as it don't hang there long enough to spoil in the sun.'

'It'll be down when its friends come round enough to take it away.' With that he heaved the yelling and kicking 'gunman' over his head and hung him from a peg sticking from the door-frame. Hooked with the suspenders of his pants, rocking with his squirming and yelling, the man was held secure on the peg.

Webb shook the liveryman's hand. 'His friends will come round in a bit and they may let him down. If they don't, just shoot him and drag him over to the undertaker's.'

The old man grinned and nodded.

'Get me down from here, you old coot,' screamed the man.

The liveryman scratched his head and watched Webb walk across the street, his bundle of pelts on his shoulder. He shook his head.

'I ain't tall enough ner strong enough to get you down,' he told the dangling man. 'Your buddies just have to come to an' climb up there an' get you. Until then, be my guest.' Cackling, the old man turned and disappeared into the stables.

THREE

It was five days before Lightning Head led his small band of warriors into their village. High in the canyon country, situated on a broad mesa, over which a small river cascaded from the mountains above, the village lay along the water utilizing the stand of pinion and pine as windbreaks against the cold winds that came down during the winter months.

Lightning Head was war chief of the village of fifty males, women and children. Ponies were kept close to the village, willingly so, on account of the lush growths of rich grass and plenty of water. There were many lodges, however some were double, so that elderly parents of either the squaw or her husband could be cared for.

Watchers on the mesa edge saw the returning band and, before Lightning Head rode into the village, the message had already been spread that they were returning. A lage crowd awaited near the chief's lodge, eager to see the returning warriors.

White Bear, the chief of the tribe, waited before his lodge, wearing his ceremonial bonnet and, about his neck, a large strand of bear teeth. Early in his maturity he had fought and slain a huge mountain grizzly. The

21

strand of teeth, strung on a leather cord was the symbol of his manhood, and his adult name became White Bear in honor of his bravery and fortitude. He stood, elderly now, but with a face that was a picture of pride, sternness and maturity to be reckoned with as long as he was chief. He watched Lightning Head lead the small band of warriors into the village and approach him. His eyes dwelled upon the white boy, riding astride the pony before the war chief.

Lightning Head slid from the back of the pony, leaving Billy astride. 'I greet my chief with pleasure to see him.'

'I see you, Lightning Head. You were successful in your journey? You found buffalo we can get for our winter food?'

Lightning Head bowed his head. 'Yes, my chief. At least ten suns from this village is a small valley. In it is a herd of buffalo we can slaughter and bring much meat back to our village.'

'It is good. Rest yourself and then come to my lodge for a council.' He looked at the white boy.

'Who is this you have brought with you? Is he a warrior of his tribe?' A small twist of the chief's lips and a twinkle of his otherwise stern eye accompanied his words.

'I captured this white boy and brought him. My wife needs another hand with her work and he will be a strong helper – with some encouragement and training.' Lightning Head turned and, taking Billy by the arm, tugged him from the pony.

Billy staggered. He was exhausted from the long, five-day travel astride the pony. Twice he had tried to escape when they camped for the night. Each time he attempted escape, he was captured within a few yards of the camp. The first time, as he was returned to camp, Lightning

Head turned him over his knees, pulled down his overalls, and spanked his rear until it was red. Billy squirmed and yelled, but did not lose his defiance.

The second time he escaped deep in the night. It was past midnight and the camp-fire was only a bed of glowing coals, when he crawled from his blanket, which they had tossed to him the first night. He quietly and slowly crept from the camp on hands and knees and when he rose to run, a tall, scowling night guard was standing over him. He was taken back into the camp and again spanked, even more severely than before. Then his hands were tied before him and his legs tied and anchored to the nearest tree. Before they broke camp the next morning Lightning Head came and untied his hands and handed him a rabbit leg for his breakfast. And talked to him.

'You cannot escape us,' he said softly, his eyes fixed intently on Billy's. 'We are alert, we are wise to the ways of captives and each time you try to escape, your punishment will be greater. Now, it will be better for you to act like a man, come quietly with us and when we arrive in our village you will live in my lodge and work for my squaw. She has been sick and needs someone to carry things for her. If you don't become wise and save yourself from punishment, I will turn you loose and let my braves use you for target practice. Do you understand?'

Billy sullenly stared back at the war chief. Finally he nodded. 'I'll not try to escape from you again, on the trail. But I make no promise after I get there.' He stared defiantly into the Indian's face.

Lightning Head's lips twisted in a slight smile.

'You just might make a great warrior, white boy. Time will tell.'

*

Billy stared at the elderly chief, silently admiring the multicolored head dress, the softly worked skins draped over the old man's shoulder. There were bright beads on his moccasins, and his hands held a carved totem of some type.

'You make a slave of this white boy?' White Bear questioned the war chief. Billy, not knowing the language, heard only guttural sounds and, to him, unintelligible utterances.

'I will give him to my squaw. She will train him in the work that boys do in the village. He will live in my lodge.'

Several youths of apparently Billy's age, crowded to the forefront of the gathering and stared at the white boy with curiosity. One, slightly taller than Billy, sneered at him. He said something aside to a companion and they laughed. Billy glared back at them. He had no idea what had been said, but he would take no bullying. He held the boy's gaze until the lad dropped his eyes.

'We will talk at the council fire this afternoon,' the old chief told Lightning Head. 'We will discuss your finding the buffalo, and what you will do with the white boy.' The old man looked steadily around him. 'Welcome home to all who were with the war chief. I congratulate you on your success.' With that he turned and entered his lodge, which was by far the most elaborate and the largest in the village.

A woman, dressed in beautifully made skins and bead-worked pantaloons, reached out and touched him. Lightning Head nodded.

'This is Bright Willow, my wife. You will go with her to my lodge and she will feed you and give you some clothes that are fitting for a boy in our village. Go now, with her.'

The pressure on his arm was gentle and as he looked into her face he saw a kind smile upon her face.

'You come,' she murmured and tugged at him. Billy hesitated a moment and then followed her. At the edge of the crowd was a slim woman, who watched closely as the white boy was led away from the chief's lodge. She followed them quietly, slipping away from the other women who had stood during the chief's welcome to the returning braves. Her eyes never left the form of the white boy and after he disappeared into the lodge of the war chief, she took some sewing from a bag she carried, and sat beneath a tree, watching the lodge.

Bright Willow motioned Billy to sit and in a moment handed him a bowl of stew. He looked at her and, recalling tales he had heard of Indians eating their dogs, glanced up at her. She smiled at him.

'I speak little English. My husband speak good English. But we will understand each other.' She nodded toward the bowl. 'Is good. Is what you call squirrel stew. You eat. Good for you.'

Billy was hungry after meager meals during the long five days to the village. He took her at her word and began eating the stew, taking lumps of meat out of the bowl with his fingers, finally taking the bowl to his mouth and draining it. Holding it, he looked up at her questioningly and she laughed softly.

'All boys hungry much time,' she said as she filled his bowl again.

Billy did not forget his vow to escape from the village and to find his way back through the mountains and canyons to his uncle's house in Denver. Clarence was his father's uncle, but Billy always called him 'uncle' out of politeness. He was certain that Clarence had had men out looking for him. His thoughts stayed closely and painfully to the last scene he had of his parents and his home, his father lying inert in the field back of the cabin, his mother falling beneath a hatchet blow by a brave. Then the smoke swirling from the doors and windows of the cabin and, he assumed, from burning barn and sheds. This was grim in his memory and his thoughts, and he was unforgiving. His parents had done nothing to the Indians. In fact, had invited some, from time to time, to eat with them when they were passing through. But Lightning Head and his braves were out to pillage and kill any whites they came across in their hunt for buffalo. He did not forget or forgive, but awaited an opportunity to escape from the village. He was determined not to be captured again, and bided his time.

The children of the village were happy, laughing, playing, teasing one another. The large boy who had sneered at Billy made it his pleasure to seek Billy out and push him or trip him, even when the white boy had been invited into a game of 'kick ball', or in foot races to determine the fleetest of foot. Another game they played was jumping over a barrier which was raised after each jump, to see finally just how high one might go. Billy found that he could jump with the best of them. None of the Indian children except the one who sneered at him, challenged him. Billy had no experience of being scorned by those of his own age, and continued to back away from the boy.

On a particular day the boys erected the jump poles and with gestures invited Billy to join them. They were dressed in breech-clouts made of soft deerskin, the rest of the body bare to the sun and elements. They were tanned deeply and consequently, Billy looked pale as he approached them for the first time, wearing a breech-clout made for him by Bright Willow. They pointed and laughed, especially the large boy, whose name was Big Foot, due to the size of his feet.

Bright Willow was working nearby, tanning a large deer hide, removing the fat and hairs. She spoke softly to Billy.

'They ask you to jump pole with them. Is good. You can jump.'

Billy was hesitant and then nodded to the boys that he would join them. The poles were set up and the first horizontal pole, to be leaped, was set knee high. The boys lined up and took turns leaping across the pole. If one struck the pole and knocked it off the uprights, he was out of the game.

'White boy cannot jump,' Big Foot commented with a snicker, glancing at his companions.

'At least I won't be held back by big feet,' Billy said. The boys did not know what he said, but Bright Willow lowered her head in a silent laugh. Billy seemed able to meet them on equal terms. He approached the pole and leaped it lightly.

The horizontal pole was raised to the thigh height. Two of the shorter boys failed to make the leap and struck the pole. They were out of the game, and stood along the sideline, yelling and laughing at those still jumping. Billy and Big Foot both cleared the pole and were ready for the next jump. There were only four of them in the contest.

The pole was raised waist high. The two other boys both leaped first, and only one cleared the pole. Big Foot hooted at Billy and, running, leaped the pole. The onlookers held their breaths. One heel scraped the pole. It jiggled and appeared ready to fall, when it righted itself and Big Foot was clear.

The pole was raised chest high. Billy eyed it warily. He had leaped barn gates and rail fences nearly that high. But he knew it was difficult. The one boy knocked the

pole down as he went over it, and was out. Billy was next.
He moved up to the pole and measured it against his
height. It struck him across the center of his chest. Big
Foot jeered and called loudly aside to his friends, point-
ing at Billy. He must have said something derisive about
Billy's ability, for they all snickered along with Big Foot.

Billy backed off. He crouched and dashed toward the
pole, and Big Foot reached out and pushed him slightly
as he prepared to leap. His balance was destroyed and he
crashed chest high into the pole, knocking it down and
one of the uprights with it. Angry, he turned to Big Foot,
his caution cast aside, but before he could attack the
bully, Lightning Head stepped up from where he had
been quietly watching the contest.

He seized Big Foot and shook him, speaking angrily to
him and forced him to replace the upright and the pole.
He motioned Billy to one side.

'Big Foot cheated you. You get another chance. But he
will jump first. You wait. Be ready.'

Billy was still angry, but he nodded and stood aside,
his ire slowly subsiding. He watched as Big Foot sullenly
replaced the upright and the pole across. He stepped
back and motioned for Billy to jump, his mouth twisted
in a grimace and his black eyes glaring at the white boy.
Lightning Head shook his head.

'No. You cheated and all saw you. Now, you jump first,
and all will watch to see if you cheat again. A warrior does
not cheat his own people or companions. Maybe some
other tribe, but not his own. Now, jump and act like a
man!'

Big Foot glared at the war chief. His father was in no
senior position in the tribe, and held only a vote in the
council. But this was the tribe's war chief chastising him.
He knew if he did not do as told, he would be turned

over to his father for discipline, and he knew his father
could be stern. He turned and faced the jump pole and
made no further overtures toward Billy.

Eyeing the jump pole carefully, he backed off and
then raced forward. A few feet before the pole was
reached he launched himself into the air and leaped
yelling as he did so. But one toe caught under the horizontal pole and knocked it off the uprights. He had not
cleared it and now only Billy was left in the contest.

The horizontal pole was in place again and Lightning
Head nodded to Billy. 'You jump now. It is your last
chance.'

Billy once again approached the pole and measured
himself against its height. He backed off several feet and
stood, concentrating. Gathering himself he ran with lithe
strides until just before the pole and then leaped. He
drew himself into a tight ball, clearing the bar and then
landed lightly on his feet beyond it.

The gathering of youths yelled and clapped. Several
adults had gathered to watch the contest, smiled and
nodded as the white boy did something none of the
others had been able to do – clear the pole at its highest
position.

Lightning Head had remained to see the outcome.
He came over and clapped Billy on the shoulder. 'You
made a fine jump, Billy. I propose an Indian name for
you.' He turned to the crowd, his hand still on Billy's
shoulder. 'From this day on, this white boy will have a
new name, according to our tribal custom. He will now
be known as "Leaping Deer".' He held Billy's arm high
and said to the crowd, 'See before you a boy with a new
name. He is now "Leaping Deer".'

There were laughing and calls to Billy. Several braves
came forward and solemnly shook his hand, and said his

name in their language, which Billy was beginning to understand. He was embarrassed at so much formal attention to what he thought of as a simple act. But at least he smiled and nodded and said in their language, haltingly, 'I am honored by the new name.'

Bright Willow had come to do handwork and watch the young people in their exercises and play. She stood, now, smiling at Billy. Her white son, whose body was slowly turning a soft tan under the sun and elements, brought her pride. He was going to make a fine brave.

Big Foot, filled with jealous anger at being bested by Billy in the pole-jump contest, stood glaring at the white boy. Billy returned his gaze unflinchingly. He knew the time would come when he would have to fight Big Foot. He was not afraid and, after winning the jumping contest, felt more confident of himself and his position in the village, especially among the village children.

Standing in the shade of one of the closer lodges, a woman, dressed in better skins and clothing than most of the other women, eyed Billy closely. A slight smile was on her lips. She watched him as he walked away with some of the children for another game, her eyes lingering on him. After a few moments of watching the boy, she turned and entered her lodge.

FOUR

Charlie Webb walked into the saloon the morning following his talk with Clarence Harris. The owner was sitting at a table near the back of the room, sipping a cup of coffee and reading a month-old copy of *The Atlantic Monthly*. He glanced up at Webb and waved him to his table.

'Had your morning java yet?' he asked the mountain man.

Webb paused. 'I just come from the eatery in the hotel. But I'll take a cup with you.' He walked to the end of the bar where coffee-pot and cups were sitting, along with some biscuits and a plate of cookies. He took a biscuit and a cup of coffee and returned to the table, seating himself across from Clarence.

After a bit of talk Clarence looked at him and set his cup on the table.

'Have you thought about what I asked you to do about finding my nephew's boy?'

Webb eyed him silently, sipping the strong black brew from the cup. 'I thought about it a lot. The only sizable Indian village is about fifty-sixty miles north and west, up in the canyon country. Pretty far in and hard to get to.

31

Old Chief White Bear keeps a pretty tight rein on his braves. But, who's to say? They may have broke away and went on a rampage on their own. Any Indian brave is his own boss. He can stay in the village or he can leave. And if a bunch of them decide to go out and do some devilment, the chief may not agree, but he can't keep them in, if they're a mind to go.'

Clarence nodded slowly. 'I know that, Charlie. And I was wondering if you could think of a way to see if it was some of his braves that went through and burned my nephew's place. And maybe carried off his boy, Billy.'

Webb eyed him and nodded slowly. 'That's a pretty big order, Clarence. But, yes, I'll have a look-see. I'll need some equipment, though, and grub for a month, maybe two. It won't be an easy thing to get him out of the camp if he is there. And it will take time.'

The saloon owner took a cigar from his vest pocket, clipped the end, lighted it and had it going before he answered. Then he nodded.

'Charlie, if anyone can do it, you can. Get the boy back and I'll make it worth your time and effort. Get whatever you need from the mercantile. How about horses?'

Webb nodded. 'I don't have a horse. I keep a pack mule and he's in your corral back of the livery. I'll need a good strong horse, and another for the boy, as well as my mule.'

'I rounded up what I could find of Walt's horses. They're in the livery-stable corral. I'm goin' to sell them to the army and bank the money in case you find the boy. There's several good animals there and a couple Walt had broken to ride. You may have to iron out the creases out of the one you take, for it ain't been rode for a spell.'

Webb rose and stretched. Clarence noted for the first time that he wore a gunbelt with a weapon on his right side. It appeared to be a .45 Colt and the butt was smooth from wear and care. Clarence also saw that he carried a knife in a sheath opposite his pistol.

'Guess I'll mosey over and get that equipment we talked about, Clarence, and I'll take a look at the hosses.' They both moved to the batwing door and stood looking out.

A tall, thin individual, dressed in what might be termed 'gambler black', stood just outside the door, leaning against the wall, seemingly interested in nothing in particular. He wore twin sixes and his long, black coat-tails were swept back, clearing the butts of his pistols. Webb turned and looked at Clarence.

'Do you know him?'

Clarence shook his head. 'Nope. Can't say I do. But he looks like he's waiting for something to happen."

Just then the three who had accosted Webb over his pelts came around the corner of the saloon and stood, grinning and spitting. It was obvious that it was a set-up.

'I think he's waiting for me to come out,' Webb said. 'Guess I'd better oblige them. Where's the back door?'

Clarence looked at him and grinned, then nodded. 'Good idea, Charlie. Just back of the bar and down the hall past my office. It opens out onto an alley that leads around to the right of the building.'

Webb nodded and left the saloon owner at the door, while he crossed the saloon, exited through the side door and disappeared from Clarence's sight. He eased from the saloon into the alley and paused, looking about. There was no one around at this time of day. For a few moments he stood just beyond the sight of the dark-clad gunman. He eased his sixgun in the leather and, taking a deep breath, stepped out of the alley and faced the front of the saloon.

Moving quickly, he unsheathed his knife and threw it unerringly to sink into the weathered siding beside the stranger with a penetrating 'slap'. The gunman whirled and, seeing Webb, stabbed down for his sixgun butts, to see himself facing the menacing bore of Webb's leveled pistol. He paused, his face blanched, his eyes glaring with anger at being stymied at his own game.

The three at the far end of the building, waiting for Webb to step from the saloon, gaped with open mouths at the sudden appearance of the mountain man.

'You lookin' for me?' Webb asked the dark-clad stranger.

He had to give the man credit for coolness. His stance relaxed and he flicked a thin smile on his thin lips. His hand eased and dangled at his side. He nodded slightly.

'You treated these friends of mine badly last night. You took their pelts they had worked so hard to accumulate. And you roughhoused them without reason. They have asked me to intervene further on their behalf.'

He talks like a schoolteacher, or a lawyer, the thought ran through Webb's mind. He holstered his sixgun.

'Your so-called friends are lying through their teeth. I worked all winter collecting those plews. My mark is on each one of them. I'm selling them to the mercantile this morning. Now, you can take it or leave it, but either way, you're in deep water if you are going to try to take the skins from me.'

The man eyed him. 'My name is Jed Hunter. I expect you have heard of me. I was close to Sam Bass during his heyday. When I give my word to do something, it's done. I gave my friends my word.'

Webb shrugged. 'Never heard of you. Who you ran

with on the owlhoot means nothing to me. Now, come on down to the street off the porch and make your play. I ain't much on talking.'

Hunter hesitated a moment and then came carefully down to the street, never taking his eyes from the big mountain man.

Facing Webb, he shrugged his shoulders to loosen the muscles and flexed his fingers. Webb noted they were thin and white, not brown and calloused as would be those of one accustomed to working under the elements of heat, wind and rain.

'Draw!' Hunter exploded coarsely, his hands sweeping down to his gun butts. As he did so, one of the men standing at the further end of the building reached for a pistol in his belt. An ominous double click sounded and he whirled to look into the round, black bore of Clarence Harris's double-barrelled twelve-gauge shot-gun.

'You all just stay put,' Harris said, his voice cold and his eyes glinting down the barrels at them. 'Charlie Webb never cheated anyone in his whole life. You are tryin' to steal something that ain't yours. So you just drop your guns and line up against the wall until this fracas is over.'

Hunter's eyes narrowed. He signaled to Webb that the man was going to draw. As the gunman's pistol cleared leather, Webb drew and fired. Hunter's slugs whistled past his ears. Hunter staggered back his guns falling from his hands, as he grabbed at his belly where Webb's bullet had entered, destroying all tissue and ripping his intestines apart. He raised his face and glared at Webb and then toppled backwards into the dust of the street. He stiffened and quivered momentarily, then relaxed into the eternal darkness of death.

FIVE

Webb dismounted and tied his horse to a rail fence some distance from the pile of ashes, partly burned logs and the still upright chimney of what had been the home of Walt Harris and his family. A pack mule and another horse were tethered to his saddle horn. He gazed about for several minutes, listening, taking in the scene that remained, telling of an energetic man who had labored for his family, carved a living out of the wilderness and died a tragic and violent death for all his labors. He saw the two mounds and crosses in a small flat area, back of the cabin ashes; the graves of Walt and Mary Harris. But for a quirk of circumstances there was not a third grave, telling where their eight-year-old son, Billy, might lie. Webb grimaced. The grave might have been a better place for the boy, rather than the life as a slave in some Indian village.

Shaking his head in sympathy, Webb walked towards what had at one time been a house and a home. He walked slowly, eyes taking in the ground, the rail fence before the cabin, which, oddly enough, had not been torn apart. Harris had left a large live-oak tree in front of the cabin and here Webb saw an arrow sticking from the bole. Part of a tack shed had failed to burn and sticking in one side were two more arrows.

Obviously the marauding Indians had not all carried rifles, or the muskets they had acquired from battlefields and raided ranches. Some had relied upon their more trusted weapons, the stout war bows-and-arrows fashioned with hand-shaped points of metal. Webb tugged the arrow from the tree and looked at it thoughtfully.

He was aware that there were Navajo in the southern portions of the Colorado territory. But there had been little trouble in recent months, the units of General Sherman's armies having brought, at least, a partial peace to the area. He turned the arrow in his hands. Tribes who manufactured their own arrows used styles and coloring of the shaft which told of their origin, if you were schooled enough in Indian warfare to know the differences. Webb had been taught by his mountain mentors the various signs that would indicate the tribe of the Indian carried it. That particular arrow was used by a Ute brave.

He walked over to the remaining wall of the shed and examined the two arrows embedded in the planks. They were of the same tribe. He paused and looked about him thoughtfully. The Utes had been peaceful for the past few years. They were not a warrior tribe primarily, as were other Indians of the plains and mountains. But that was not to say a roaming band of Utes had not found this isolated ranch and, for hatred of all whites, or perhaps out of pure thrill of destruction, had killed the owners and laid waste to the buildings.

Webb turned and looked out over the nearer pastures, now lush with grass. He caught a glimpse of cattle in the distance. Apparently the Indians were not, at this point, hunting for food, or they undoubtedly would have killed and butchered the beef, or driven them before them to their village.

In the far distance he caught a quick glance of a small herd of wild horses disappearing beyond the mist of a high mesa. Any of Harris's horses left by Clarence and his friends, would have become wild, even joined or taken by the wild bunch.

He sat on the top rail of a fence and noticed the lip of a well, back of what had been the home. Harris had been industrious, had built a home, fenced his land, dug a well. He filled a blackened pipe with tobacco, tamped it firmly in the bowl, lighted it and puffed until he had it going. What had been in the mind of the white man when he looked up from where he was probably working, and saw an attacking warrior swinging a hatchet at his head, or releasing an arrow at him? Webb shook his head. The frontier was wild and hard, even harsh, and it took courage to stay and labor to be able to view a life-work. Harris had been such a man.

Now, he thought, what became of the boy? Did the lad hide and run and attempt to return the rough fifty miles over canyon and ridge, valley and mountain to Denver? Did he become the victim of a hungry cougar, or had he been mauled and killed by a frightened bear sow, when he came too close to her cubs? Or was he carried away by the marauders and was now in an Indian village as a slave? Webb rose and began to cast about for some sign. Had the boy been killed here? He spent an hour searching for the boy's body, cloth remaining over animal-strewn bones – any indication that the boy had been killed along with his parents. He found none.

There was little or no sign for him to follow. It had been over two months since the raid. Wind, rain, the concerned men with Clarence Harris searching, trampling about, all tended to destroy any trails left by the Indians. Webb widened his circle of searching and found the hoof-prints where the Indians had crossed the creek, entering the pasture that led up to the house. On the rail fence surrounding what had been their large garden, he found blood on the top pole. Finally, a half-mile from the house, he found tracks leading away from the ranch. Going back and mounting his horse, he followed the signs into the canyon back of the property. All at once he realized the band was heading west and north, deeper into the canyon country, toward the rearing shoulders of mountains. He paused and watered his horse at a small stream, studying the lay of the land before him. The band was heading for their village, he was certain. What tribe was up there in the high meadows and misty canyons? He nodded to himself.

Old Chief White Bear. He had dodged the armies attempting to round up his tribe and bundle them into a reservation to the south. The wily old chief had escaped them thus far. But he was up there somewhere. And suddenly Webb was certain that Billy Harris was there, working under the sharp eyes of some squaw.

Studying the sky, Webb realized there were only a few hours of daylight left. He returned to the burned-out ranch and there, beside the small creek, made camp for the night. Visiting the well he found that it had not been destroyed, but that the well-bucket on the end of a rope was still secured to a hook in the field-rock rim. He lowered and filled the bucket, lifting it to the surface. The water was clear and, as he drank, sweet and refreshing. He filled a canteen for the evening and turned the animals loose in the pasture, knowing they would not stray away from the field of the lush grass.

He sat late beside his camp, gazing into the dimming

coals of his fire, sipping on coffee from time to time. He was satisfied that the Indians had carried Billy Harris away. Now, his job was to find him and somehow get him back to his kin in Denver. This thought paramount in his thinking, he rolled into his blankets and was soon relaxed in a deep sleep.

Old Chief White Bear called a council one morning several weeks following Lightning Head's announcement that there were buffalo for the taking in a small valley about ten suns away from the village.

'I have had a vision,' he told the circle of the council, made up of elders of the village, as well as the tribal war chief, the shaman and a woman of indeterminable age, a soothsayer.

'I have visited the valley our war chief, Lightning Head, told of, and found in my dream more than enough buffalo to give us meat for the winter. My signs say that we should go soon, before the cold winds come, make the meat for our village, and return. My vision told me that this was a good thing. I wait to hear what the council believes.'

The thought of a buffalo hunt, with meat plentiful for the winter months met with excited approval from the council members. 'Then,' said the chieftain, 'so it will be. We will make ready and leave immediately. Everyone will go, for many hands will make the work easier and quicker, and we will be back in our lodges before the Moon of the Cold Winds comes.'

The news was spread. Within hours the entire village, from the eldest to the youngest, was packed and ready to go. The women bundled clothes and sleeping mats, flaying knives and cooking pots, taking what they would need to process the kill. Older boys were assigned to the horses, driving those not ridden, forming travois to carry supplies, bedding, and to provide transportation for some who were too elderly to walk the distance. It was an exhilarated, laughing, talking village – setting out on a journey which would assure them of necessities for the long months of winter certain to begin before too many weeks.

Billy Harris was among the horse handlers. He had learned to ride a paint pony, using only a hackamore and pressure of his body to guide the animal. He had formed a friendship with a girl two years older than he, whose willingness to teach him the ways of life in the village had made the transition easier. He was learning the language and could now converse fairly well in their tongue. A bright, intelligent boy he did not dwell on the fact of his parents' death, but on the fact that he was alive, fed and treated well, since the Indian woman, Bright Willow, had received him as a gift from her husband, Lightning Head. She had been kind, tender at moments, but was a woman of the village, and therefore under her husband's orders. That was to teach the white boy the ways of the tribe. He had duties he must perform and she, patiently, drilled him in their performance until he met her goals. He carried water, brought wood for the fires, practised the language under her tutorage, and quickly became receptive to all that was required of him, or which he found necessary to learn.

He was accepted among the children, whose playing, racing, wrestling and imitations of the adult warriors was a constant daily exercise. He, having already ridden his father's horses, was found to be one whose rapport with animals was greater than most. The paint pony was a present to him from Lightning Head, when the village war chief noted that he had a way with animals. It took only a few times mounted with the simple hackamore, to learn the knee and thigh pressures that would also guide the animal. It was natural, when time came for the village boys to handle the horse herd, that Billy was assigned to the task.

The girl's name meant Laughing Waters, undoubtedly on account of her laughing nature and her giggling when she was amused. She quickly became Billy's friend, and it was with her and from her that he increased his knowledge of the language and the ways of life in the village.

As he left, with the other youths, to round up the herd and begin the drive, following the slowly traveling village, she caught his glance, laughed and tossed her black hair. He waved back and then began the time-consuming task of rounding up the stubborn horses and getting them herded in the direction indicated by the war chief.

Lightning Head stood at the edge of the now deserted village and looked into the mountains beyond. It was over six or seven suns back to the ranch that he and his braves had destroyed, killing and scalping the rancher and his wife. There was an uneasiness in his mind. Someone, he thought, is looking for the boy. Someone coming, who has the wisdom of tracking and is wily enough to find the village and exact revenge for the work of the hunters returning from their search for buffalo.

He called two of the braves who had been on the hunt and were involved in the destruction of the ranch. He gave them instructions to go back over the way the group had traveled, watching for whatever it might be that was causing his anxiety. With the village strung out over several miles in travel, it would be vulnerable to a quick attack and lives would be lost. The two braves listened, mounted their ponies and disappeared up the canyon, following the way along which they had arrived several weeks previously.

Lightning Head was relieved. If there was danger for the village from that direction, it would be seen and he would be warned and prepared.

SIX

Webb rolled out of his blankets at first light. Dawn was an hour away, but here in the mountains first light came gradually, starting about four o'clock in the morning, depending upon the weather. He lay still and listened. Only the sound of the wind in the trees, a few birds awakening with sleepy chirps. He heard the snuffle and stir of his horses and the pack mule in the small cul-de-sac where he had hobbled them. There was lush grass, with a small stream running through it. He heard nothing nearby that should not be abroad. Earlier in the evening he had heard the cough of a panther, but it was not close. Coyotes along the flat mesa had echoed each other during the early hours, but, their hunting satisfactory, their voices had ceased.

He rolled out of his blanket, and taking up each boot, turned them upside down and shook them. A small timber-rattler might use one for a warm bed during the chilly hours of the night. Satisfied that they were free of any creepy items, he tugged them on, sat up, pulled his belt tightly about his waist and rose. He checked his hat and finding it unoccupied by any visitors come during the night, put it on. Leaving the campsite, he went to the

44

small cove where he had hobbled the animals and
checked to assure himself that they were there and
unharmed. He made certain they were able to reach the
water, then returned to the campsite and prepared his
first meal of the day. It could be a long day, for he
expected to follow the slight tracks he had found until he
could fathom just where they were leading.

His meal over and the fire doused, he brought up the
horses and pack mule and prepared for the day's trek.
He looked about him to make certain he had left nothing behind, then mounted and guided his horse out of
the small cove where they had spent the night. A few
hundred yards from where he had camped, he had
found prints of unshod horses. As there were no wild
bands in the immediate area, he thought it very likely the
tracks were made by those who had destroyed the Harris
ranch, and had taken the boy captive.

Webb was an excellent tracker. He had been in the
mountains long enough to have learned signs. Broken
twigs from bushes and trees, overturned stones, a hoof-
print in soft ground or along a stream. There were many
things to indicate the presence and passage of animals
and humans, especially humans. Even, he thought wryly,
the Indian, believed to be so wily in leaving so little
evidence of his passing, was careless at times. His eyes
were constantly alert, watching, noting the lay of the
land, the direction of the scant sign of hoof-prints which
he was following. From time to time he mounted a rise
halted just behind the crest, tethered the animals and
carefully approached the crest of the slope. He removed
his hat and raised himself just enough to see beyond the
crest. Sweeping the entire area carefully, he watched for
several minutes, seeing no movement that might have
been Indians along the mountainside, and the edge of a

flat mesa, which stretched blue and rough for a long distance. This he did several times during the day and the second day as well. On the morning of the third day, he lost the signs of the warrior band passing this way. It was a long hunt until he found it, several hundred yards from where he had spent the night. Weather in the mountains had erased much of the sign and it was now very difficult to follow.

Shadow Walker and One Who Runs were the two Indians sent back along the trail, to make certain no one was following their signs to the village.

They were eager to do their leader's bidding and spent careful time in watching the back trail, moving slowly, taking advantage of any growth that would hide their presence. It was on the third day that they had been on the trail when Shadow Walker {named so because he had insomnia and wandered around at night, sleepless}, held up his hand and halted One Who Runs where he was.

'I see movement ahead.'

'Is it White Eyes, spying on our village?' asked his companion. Shadow Walker shook his head.

'I do not know. I saw only a small movement of a juniper. Something must have moved through and made it shake.'

One Who Runs, named so because he was the designated runner to take messages from Chief White Bear to other tribal leaders in times of emergency, shook his head. 'Wind, a bear digging for grubs, many things can make a bush shake. Do you see any animals?'

Shadow Walker held up a hand for silence. He had heard something that was foreign to the area, the scrape of a hoof on a rock, the deep breathing of a horse as it climbed the side of a coulee.

'There is someone out there following the way we came after we taught the white eyes a lesson for trying to make a farm out of our hunting grounds,' he whispered. 'Be quiet and watch.'

Then, at least three miles away, Charlie Webb's bulky form appeared for an instant and then was gone. Shadow Walker sighed and turning, looked at his companion. 'A white man is following our signs. He is very good, for the signs would all be nearly gone by now.'

'Do we surprise and kill him?'

Shadow Walker shook his head. 'No, we will watch and move back and around him, and follow *his* sign. When he makes his fire for evening meal, we will attack.'

One Who Runs nodded after some moments of thought. 'It is a good plan,' he grunted. 'We will take his hair back and give it to Lightning Head. He will be pleased.'

Charlie Webb was aware that he must be nearing the Indian village encampment. He was also aware that for two days he had been followed by one or more trackers. They were wily, their movements hidden; he had caught only a fleeting glimpse now and then of movement, a shadow within a shadow where normally shadows were without movement. Then those furtive 'corners of the eye' appearances were gone. For a full day now he had seen nothing, nor heard nothing.

As he rose from his blankets on the morning of what would be his sixth day on the trail he realized that this might be the day his followers made themselves known. Undoubtedly they had circled and would be coming up from back of him, attempting to surprise in their attack.

He ate a cold breakfast, drank cold water from a small stream, where he filled his canteen for the day. He brought his horses into the campsite and groomed them, all the time listening, watching, knowing and feeling that those following him were close by.

He had chosen his campsite carefully, with a large fallen tree at his back. He moved the animals to the center of the area and mounted. As he lifted the reins of his mount, his attackers struck!

An arrow whizzed past his ear to thunk into the log of the tree beside him. He released the other animals and yelled, kicking the nearest and causing it to jerk away and run to the other side of the small clearing. The mule brayed as an arrow grazed its hip and then followed the other animal from the center of the attack.

Webb swung from the saddle, jerking his rifle from its sheath. He levered a shell into the breech and shoved his mount away from him, then he crouched and faced the direction from which the arrow had come. As he did so Shadow Walker burst from the cover of a low-spread aspen and leaped at him. The Indian screamed and, brandishing a hatchet, gathered during some raid upon white settlements or ranches, swung at Webb and immediately reversed for a repeated swing. The hatchet blade swished close to Webb's shoulder, and then his 1850 Henry Repeater rifle spat its round at the Indian's belly. The ball entered and knocked the yelling Indian flat. He attempted to rise but Webb had jacked another shell into the chamber and fired again, a red hole appearing in the Indian's forehead.

Webb levered his rifle again and whirled about in time to catch One Who Runs as the brave dropped his bow and launched himself bodily at the white man. The weight of the Indian threw Webb back against the trunk of the tree he had kept at his back. The scent of the Indian's body, rancid grease, bodily odour from days without bathing, the very essence of hate and excitement, assailed the white man's nostrils. But he was too busy to do more than notice the scents of the man now clasped in his huge arms, held tightly to escape the threat of a knife, gripped in the brave's hand.

One Who Runs screamed in frustration, as Webb's tremendous strength bent him backwards and suddenly pinned him against the tree-trunk. The knife rose suddenly and struck, penetrating Webb's sleeve and slicing into the thick part of his forearm. He winced with the pain and suddenly threw the Indian from him.

One Who Runs landed upon his back and, like a cat, was immediately on his feet and diving back toward his enemy. But Webb had had fleeting seconds of recovery, and as the Indian dived against him, drawing back the knife for another thrust, he drew his pistol and fired three rounds which sounded like one continuous roll of thunder. The Indian twisted in the air and his diving body thumped against the fallen tree-trunk, back of which Webb was crouched. All three slugs had entered his body, one tearing through his heart, ending his life before his body hit the ground.

Webb remained where he was. There had been two of the braves, but there might be more. He listened intently, and heard the birds' sounds returning. Wind in the branches of the trees above him rustled. Somewhere a squirrel chattered in annoyance. The bodies of the two Indians did not move. Either they were dead, or were very adept at achieving complete stillness.

At last the mountain man stirred. With cocked revolver he stepped quietly over to the body nearer to him, reached down and searched for a pulse in the neck.

There was none. He slipped over the log and cautiously did the same to the other body, checking for life, but keeping his weapon cocked and pressed against the Indian's head. But this one was also devoid of life. He sighed and rose. Leaning against the tree, he slipped new shells into his rifle, and checked his pistol to make certain it was fully loaded and ready for any emergency.

The horses had fled as far from the fracas as they could get, but were in sight among the trees close to the clearing. Within minutes Webb had them ready for travel. He stood, looking out over the land, searching for any movement. Apparently the chief knew he was being followed or at least sensed it. But two strong and experienced braves should be enough to eliminate any white eye attempting to follow their sign. That would have been the thinking, the mountain man surmised. After long minutes of surveying the surroundings, he mounted and, leading the other animals, moved out to find again the trail which would lead to the Ute village.

Before leaving the campsite, he removed as much sign of his having been there as possible. The bodies of the two Indians he placed behind the fallen tree that had been his barricade during the fight, and covered them with bark from the ancient tree and other debris that he found nearby. He realized it was only a measure of time before the hiding-place of the Indians would be indicated by the swirl of the vultures that would be circling the area. However, he would have a few hours of travel before someone discovered the bodies.

Finding the faint signs of the trail again, he moved away on his journey without thought of what lay behind him. Foremost was to find the village and, somehow, quietly steal the boy away.

Lightning Head sat on his pony as the village moved past him. It was a slow movement, taking an entire village through the mountains, children, women, elders, all moving at a pace which irked him, but which he knew was the way it was done.

He looked back into the mountains. Shadow Walker and One Who Runs had been gone three days. By this time they would have located and removed any danger to the village. Still, Lightning Head had an uneasy feeling. Surely they were on their way back to join the movement. The feeling grew that all was not right, but there was nothing to do about it at this point. First, get the village to the valley where the fat buffalo waited. The rest could be dealt with in the fullness of time.

SEVEN

Billy Harris was so caught up in the excitement and flurry of the village move that he had no thought of the tragedy that had led him to this place. He rode his small, piebald pony, given him by Lightning Head and, with the other boys, hazed the village horses along the track left by the moving travois and hurrying footsteps. They were so busy that even Big Foot, who had constantly harassed Billy since his coming, was too occupied to cause him any trouble.

Bright Willow, under whose care he existed and whose responsibility to her husband, the war chief, Lightning Head, was to teach and improve Billy's understanding, was too caught up in the movement of her lodge, her older parents, and two young children, to do more than glance at him when the village paused for a noon or evening meal. She was content that he was being kept occupied and looked back, now and then, to locate him through the dust haze thrown up by the movement of the village and the horse herd.

Curiously enough, the woman, who seemed always to be on the periphery of Billy's days, kept her own vigilance over the boy. One of Chief White Bear's wives, she was always near the elderly man, seeing to his needs and, during the move of the village, was in charge of his possessions, seeing that all was as he wished. Nevertheless, she was never without knowledge of where the white boy was working the horses. She made her way to the side of the long line of walkers and drawn travois' and looked to make certain Billy was safe. If any of the other wives of the old chief noticed her constant obser- vance of the white boy, they said nothing about it. It was her business. They had more to do than keep track of the boy.

The trip to the place where Lightning Head had seen the buffalo was normally of at least ten days' duration, but with the entire moving, it would be longer, because of the pauses necessary for eating and resting, the slow pace of the elderly and the arduousness of the passage over some very rough terrain. But the thought of the fat buffalo from which would come the major portion of their winter food, was enough to encourage them. The constant wear and tear of the movement wore on all, but none thought of not continuing until their goal was reached.

Charlie Webb lay in a small copse of aspen overlooking the valley before him. The village was empty. Lodges were still there, intact, telling him it was a move with an intention of returning, otherwise the lodges would have been dismantled and all usable parts taken to be utilized at the Indians' next encampment. He lay a long time watching, listening. But all sounds of an active village life were gone. There came only the sound of the wind in the trees, the raucous call of a crow signaling that however still he might lie, the telescopic eye of the bird had seen him and was notifying the world of his presence. Webb did not move. Eventually the look-out crow would forget him and stop his racket.

The village was gone. Webb was puzzled. Why? It was late in the season for such a move. The hunters should be out procuring provisions for the winter ahead. He noticed that a wide sign of the movement of the village led off toward the south and west. There were only two things that might cause an entire tribe to move lock, stock and barrel. Either the government had tired of playing around with old Chief White Bear, and had come and rounded up the entire village and was taking it to the reservation. Or there was a find of buffalo somewhere back in these hills, which they were after to supply them with enough meat and fat for the long winter months.

Buffalo was nearly hunted out. Once roaming in millions all over the West, and especially in the high plains, the magnificent beast had been decimated by white hunters, providing food for the train-gangs, and hides to sell back East. Now and then, however, some wily old bull had found a hidden valley, lush with grass, and there had led his small herd, seeking safety from the encroachment of the white hunters.

For centuries the Indian had used the buffalo for food, for material to create lodges, clothing and other uses, making the animal a living necessary item of livelihood. Now, the beast was rarely found and the hunters were obliged to hunt far and wide, and often came up empty handed.

That must be the reason for the entire village to move. Somewhere out there among the mountains in some hidden valley or on some high mesa, there must be something to draw an entire village. And, to Webb's thinking, they must have located buffalo. It was time for 'meat gathering'. These were not tribes to plant corn or

pumpkins or squash to dry for the winter food. There
must be meat, fat to cook with, tendons to sew with,
bones to crack and draw out the sweet marrow. He cast
about, moving around the village and in a short while
found the signs he had suspected. Yards wide, showing
unshod pony-hoof prints, tracks of travois being dragged
behind ponies trained for such work. Moccasin foot-
prints, both mature and young. He nodded and rising
from his examination of sign, looked into the distance,
searching the direction in which the signs pointed. The
village was out there, moving. And the white boy would
be with it, by now inured to whatever tasks his captor set
him to.

No longer hurrying, but keeping to swales, following just
below the ridge lines, Webb came upon the village the
day it arrived at the valley where Lightning Head had
found the buffalo. He watched as the village spread out,
choosing a wide, flat place, where a small stream marked
one side, the traveling tepees were raised, fires built and
horses corralled. They had found their 'epi', their huge
woolly prey, which would push away the haunting spectre
of famine. They would eat well when the snows were
deep around the hogans.

Billy Harris liked working with the horses. He had a
way with animals, and could walk up to almost any pony
in the remuda and within minutes have it gentled. His
youthful opponent, Big Foot, sneered at his method and
punished his own ponies, using rough tactics in his
handling.

'White Boy knows nothing about training ponies for
use,' he laughed at Billy. His followers fell in step with
him and in many ways made the white boy's existence
among them miserable. It was following one day of work-

ing with Bright Willow that Big Foot pushed until Billy's ire was raised.

The Indian boy had watched while Billy carried water to the tepee of Bright Willow. He was busy doing menial things, wood for the fire, spreading the sleeping blankets to air, things Bright Willow gave him to do.

'You are a girl-boy,' Big Foot called to him while Billy was polishing a cooking pot. 'You do woman's work. You will never be a warrior.'

The Indian boy walked over and with one foot kicked Billy in the side as he was kneeling over his work. Billy fell to one side, dropping his clean utensil in the dirt. Now it was to be done all over again. Flushing with quick anger, he leapt to his feet and faced Big Foot.

'I do what I am told to do. You do nothing but make trouble for everyone. Leave me alone. But if you touch me again, I will fight you.'

Big Foot laughed and hooted, pointing to Billy. 'He would fight me. Yes, I will fight you.' With no further warning the larger boy leaped at Billy and, as the white boy was not yet fully risen from the ground, bowled him over again and then threw his entire body upon him. They squirmed and pushed and yelled at each other, until Billy finally, more agile than Big Foot, squirmed free and stood as the Indian boy leaped to his feet.

As Big Foot poised to launch himself again, intending to wrestle him to the ground, Billy set himself. He and his father had often wrestled and Walt Harris, having boxed some while in the army, had taught Billy some moves.

'Make a fist,' he told his son, 'if your opponent insists on fighting. And get in a quick first blow, if possible. Side-step his rushes and as he passes, plant a fist in his side. And move about, don't stand and let him make a punch-bag out of you.'

Billy remembered. As Big Foot flung himself at him, Billy slipped quickly to one side, and as the Indian boy passed him, planted a fist in his side. Big Foot staggered and fell.

The fight between the two boys drew a crowd. The other children crowded about and noisily encouraged their favorite, most of them urging Big Foot. A loud groan rose when their choice staggered and fell, yelling as Billy's fist brought pain to his ribs.

He scrambled to his feet and, snarling, rushed Billy again, who stepped back, and as the Indian boy closed with him, brought up his right fist which connected with his opponent's nose and mouth with a loud slap. Big Foot fell again, this time with blood pouring from his mashed nose and split lips.

Billy was cool. He knew he was hurting the Indian boy. He was aware that adults were coming to watch. Bright Willow was among them, concern on her face. When Big Foot came slowly to his feet, blood streaming down his face, her hands went to her mouth in surprise. She had no idea that the white boy could fight like that, and he fought strangely, with clenched fists.

Standing in the circle of children was the girl, Laughing Waters. Her face was pale and she grimaced whenever Billy fell to Big Foot's onslaughts. She, also, had noted Billy's fists and wondered if this was a white-eye way of fighting. But the thought was fleeting for she was hoping to see Billy win the fight, whatever methods he used.

Big Foot rose and wiping his face and chin with a hand, he stood glaring at the white boy. 'You fight a strange way, White Eye. Indians do not close their fists, but use forearms and elbows and knees. That is the way a real warrior fights. You are no warrior.'

Billy shook his head. 'You are right. I am not a warrior.
I am not Indian. I am of white blood. I fight as my father
taught me. Try to be friends, talk the problem out, and
shake hands. But you will not do this. So I fight you the
only way I know to fight.' Billy stood looking at Big Foot
levelly, seemingly with no fear in him.

Lightning Head came up and pushed through the
crowd. He looked at both boys, and his lips twitched in a
slight smile and then straightened sternly. He eyed Big
Foot. 'You seem to have bumped your nose and lip on
something, boy,' he said wryly. 'Now, I suggest each of
you has enough to do with the horses.' He motioned to
the crowd. 'Go back to your work. This match is over.
There is no winner or loser.'

Big Foot scowled at Lightning Head, for boys his age
did not take orders from any but their fathers. However,
he did not argue but turned and walked away,
surrounded by his circle of close friends. Lightning Head
looked at Billy, standing quietly, expecting at least a
scolding from the war chief.

'You fight well in your white man's way, Leaping Deer.'
He called Billy by the Indian name given him from his
early days with the village. 'However, you will do well to
learn the Indian way of personal combat. And the use of
Indian weapons as well. I will see that you learn the use
of the bow and arrow, the lance and the tomahawk or
hatchet. If you are to be with the Indians a long time, it
is well you learn to fight the Indian way.'

Billy nodded. 'I will be happy to learn,' he said.
Lightning Head narrowed his eyes at him and, slapping
him on the shoulder, left the area. He was thoughtful.
The white boy could learn. He was intelligent. And the
way he fought the larger boy showed skill and willingness
to use what he had learned in personal hand-to-hand

encounter. He might, just might, become a warrior.

Bright Willow was relieved that the conflict between the two youths was over and in a secret way, pleased that Billy had actually won in the encounter. She went about her chores and gave it little further thought. The strange woman who had stood on the fringe of the fight remained watching the white boy as he scurried away with the girl, Laughing Water, and some of his friends. She was pleased that Billy had proved himself capable of meeting those of his own age.

Charlie Webb's mind was in a whirl. He lay in a copse of small pine and aspen on a knoll above the small creek that threaded the edge of the Indian camp. He lay well concealed and trained his field glasses, Civil War vintage, upon the village. As he moved the lenses slowly about, shading them to make certain there was no glare from the glass to alert sharp eyes to his presence, the lenses were suddenly focused upon a woman, in well-prepared clothing. She stood looking up towards him, as though she knew he was there.

He fingered the focus gently, bringing her into clearer vision, and, startled, he removed the field glasses and rubbed his eyes. Blinking and shaking his head, he looked through the glasses again and the woman was still there, looking now to the far side of the village, where the horses were loosely corralled. He swore gently, not believing.

'My God, a white woman! And I know her.' He cast about in his memory of faces, not taking his eyes off the form framed in his glasses. It came to him.

'Sara Wilcox, by the gods! A captive of the Utes! It's been five years since you were taken!'

EIGHT

Clarence Harris turned slightly in his chair at his favorite table in the Denver saloon, and eyed the two men who entered and approached the bar. They both ordered whiskey and stood sipping it and talking quietly. But Clarence noted that the taller of the men, a silver-haired man, approaching middle years, just beginning to thicken about the waist, was busy cataloguing what he saw in the room reflected in the long mirror back of the bar.

The second man, younger in appearance, stocky and with rather sullen features, turned and leaned against the bar, boldly looking at every person in the room. Both men were armed with sixguns, riding low on the right thigh. And Clarence noted that the leather of the short man was tied about his leg, gunman style. The saloon owner felt a chill run up his spine. Here was trouble brewing. Some things would change and not necessarily for the better.

Clarence rose, went to the bar and gestured for the barkeep to fill his glass. He spoke to the taller of the two men.

'Welcome to my establishment, gentlemen,' he said,

lifting his glass. 'I presume you are new in the area.'

The tall man turned to Clarence and nodded. 'Yes. We are in Denver for the first time. I'm Roman McClure, this is my foreman, Laff Brock. You have a nice place here.'

Brock nodded curtly to Clarence and continued his surveying of the room. What's troubling him, wondered the saloon-keeper. But he returned to the man named McClure.

'Your foreman? Then you're a business man?'

McClure shook his head. 'I'm a rancher. I was told there is some good grass left here in this part of the country. I'm looking for something to settle into.'

Clarence shook his head. 'Not much around here. Back in the mountains there are some high meadows, but most of them have been taken by local ranchers and horse-breeders. Here,' he motioned to the man, 'come on over to my table and we'll talk.'

McClure eyed him and then shook his head. 'Thanks for the invite, but I'm not staying in town. I'm going to see the banker and then head out. On the way here we ran upon a place that looks just about what we want. About thirty miles back.'

A chill ran through Clarence's back. Thirty miles? That would be the distance to his brother Walt's place. But there was only the chimney standing and some fencing might remain. However, he shrugged.

'I can't imagine where that might have been.' He straightened and placed his glass on the bar. 'Whatever,' he said, 'welcome to Denver and perhaps you will find something you are looking for, although I doubt it.'

The two men had a second drink and then left the saloon. The short, stocky man identified as Brock, turned at the door and briefly looked over at Clarence. His eyes were cold and seemed to indicate that he felt

Clarence knew more about the availability of land than he had said. He followed his boss and Clarence again felt the chill. After an hour he left his table and walked out of the saloon. He crossed the street and entered the bank, a few doors away.

An elderly bank clerk, Mattie Watson, whom he had known for years, looked over and greeted him with a smile. 'Morning, Clarence,' she said. 'Don't tell me you've made so much money already you've come to make a deposit in your account.'

'No, Mattie. But I'd like a minute or two with your boss, if he's free.'

She nodded at the door leading to the banker's office. 'He's not busy right now. Go on in.'

Clarence Harris was one of the wealthy men of the town, and his deposits in the bank were regular and substantial. Clarence knocked on the door and opened it.

The banker, Will Martin, looked up from a ledger he was working on. He closed the book and leaned back, gesturing for the saloon-keeper to enter.

'Howdy, Clarence. You're up and around early today. What brings you into this establishment of evil gains, as you so often accuse it.'

Clarence grinned and took a seat beside the desk. He and Martin had come into Denver about the same time, and had known each other, doing business together, for several years. They had been at ease with each other since the very beginning of their relationship. Civic-minded, they had worked together for the betterment of the town, which had grown and prospered under their guidance, along with that of the community fathers, in other areas of interest and need.

'Will, I know you don't talk about your depositors and

your work with them. But I have a question. Did a stranger named McClure and his foreman, Brock, visit you this morning?'

Martin leaned back in his chair. He trusted Clarence Harris as no other man he knew. He eyed Clarence thoughtfully for a long moment and then nodded.

'There's no secret about his visiting me,' he said. 'And since he made no deposit of any kind, there's no secrets to be divulged. All he asked was if I was holding any mortgages that might be in trouble, or if I knew of any ranches hereabouts that might be interested in selling out. That was the extent of our talk.'

Clarence nodded. He pursed his lips a moment, frowning in thought. 'He mentioned to me that he had come on a place about thirty miles from here that he might be interested in. It sounded a lot like my brother Walt's place. But that ain't for sale, you know that. I'm keepin' it for Walt's boy, if he is ever found and brought back to us.'

Martin shook his head. 'McClure made no mention of finding any kind of place he might be interested in.' He looked thoughtfully at his friend. 'You might think of selling that property an' putting the money in a trust for his boy, in case he is found.'

Clarence shook his head. 'No, not yet. I might, if it looks like he won't be found. But I have to give Charlie Webb time to see if he can find Billy.'

The banker raised his eyebrows. 'Charlie Webb? He's looking for the boy?'

Clarence nodded.

'Well, if anyone could find him, it would be Webb. He knows these mountains like the back of his hand, and he speaks some of the tribal languages.'

Clarence sighed and rose. 'Thanks, Will. If you hear

anything that seems like McClure is moving in on property somewhere, how about letting me know? I'll make certain he ain't taking up my brother's place.'

But McClure *was* taking up Walt Harris's ranch. He left Denver and led his crew of five men to the high meadows where the lonely chimney stood thrusting its finger to the sky. Here he stopped and dismounted. He walked the area, stood looking into the far distances that stretched from the place where he stood to the blue horizons at the edges of the mesa where the Harris property ended. He nodded to Brock, his foreman.

'This is where we'll spend the winter, Laff. Get some trees cut and build a shed for the hosses and a two-room cabin for us to live in. Come spring, we'll maybe plan for a trip to that ripe little bank in Denver. In the meantime, them as are looking for us will give up the chase and we'll be ready to do a little rampaging when the winter breaks.'

Brock nodded and spat. 'This is as good a place as any to hole up,' he grunted, 'an' maybe better than most.'

McClure turned and walked back toward the chimney which spoke with a single voice that there had once been a home here. It was not the best arrangement, he thought, but it was out of the way, deep in the mountains, and winter was coming on with deep snows. Few lawmen would challenge the weather before spring, even if they had some information that the McClure gang was holed up on what was known as the Walt Harris holdings.

NINE

The village was deep into the activity of procuring meat, hides, horns, hoofs and even tails of the buffalo. Every item of the animal would be put to use, even to tendons, harvested to be used in repairing lodges, clothing and weapons. The buffalo was life to the Indian and, now that it was disappearing from the scene, when found, care was taken that every possible part of the Great Spirit's blessings would be utilized, nothing wasted.

The braves went out to the herd and, quietly slipping up close to the animals, would spear or kill one with the heavy hunting bow. The animal would run and fall and, since there was little noise, the rest of the herd would move slightly to another position and then return to their grazing. Over several days the men of the village easily garnered the best of the herd, from fat cows to young animals. The older, tougher ones would be left to the last and, if not needed, allowed to live, with the hope that they would not move from the lush grasses of the valley where they were now gathered.

Billy Harris was caught up in the busy activity of keeping ponies ready for the braves when they came in to change animals. The bigger boys, including Billy, were taken to the edge of the herd and there, with ropes around the neck of the dead animal, would drag the buffalo to the place where the squaws waited to do the butchering.

Once the squaws had the body of the buffalo, the boys and men were sent on their way. The women were the experts at skinning the animals so the hides would be intact. These were scraped, removing the fat and flesh, and then staked out in the sun to dry. Later, during the long winter days, the women would work the hides until they were soft and pliant. The present was, however, taken up with removing the best parts of the animal to be cured and held against the lean months when the snows were deep and one could move only slightly about the village.

The bigger boys were allowed to work with the squaws and pull the pelts from the bodies of the animals. Under the supervision of the women, they worked at this, and eventually in stretching and staking the hides. But every boy yearned to be at the edge of the herd, watching the braves select and bring down a chosen cow, or a young bull. They yearned for the time they would be allowed to become one of the hunters, using the bow or the spear. Guns were not used here, for it was feared the small herd would stampede at the noise. Better to quietly harvest what was needed. Perhaps the last few days might be used for sport, chasing down chosen animals, killing from the back of the pony, while riding at breakneck speed, the mount guided by the sway of the body, or the pressure of the knees and thighs.

As the village labored to replenish its food supply, Charlie Webb watched from various points above the encampment. He especially watched the activity of Sara Wilcox, for he was certain the woman he watched was she.

Watching the boys with the ponies, at the chores about the camp, Webb was never certain which was Billy Harris. Several were of the same size. While they went through their activities in the warm, early autumn sun, all were equally tanned. Perhaps the Indian boys were darker in color but, even so, Billy had tanned so well that at a distance he looked, with his hair braided back as the others were fashioned, like any Indian boy doing his chores.

It was into the third week of his arrival at the encampment that Webb made his first contact with the woman he was certain he had recognized.

It was early evening, shadows were growing long and darkness was only minutes away, when the strange woman, coming from the chief's tepee, walked slowly and thoughtfully toward the area set aside as the women's ground. Here only the women and girls were allowed at the time when nature called, or in preparation for the night. Webb had sighted the ground early in his time of surveillance. He had moved into hiding not far from the places were the women entered the grounds. On this evening he noticed the strange woman approaching. As she approached his place of concealment, he called softly so that his voice carried only a slight distance, but loud enough for it to reach her ears.

'Sara … Sara Wilcox….'

The woman jerked to a stop, her head coming up. Her eyes immediately followed the sound of his voice. All she could see was bushes and the lowering limbs of a huge pine.

'Sara … Sara Wilcox. Don't be afraid. A friend is here. Come in closer so we can talk.'

She trembled. It had been at least four years since she had heard English spoken correctly. Indian smatterings

of English words and phrases were not unusual among
the tribes. But, this was different. She stiffened and,
lowering her head, moved slowly toward where the voice
had come from.

'Sara,' his voice was low, but she heard it clearly. 'My
name is Charlie Webb. I've come to find a white boy, and
I saw you. I recognized you from Fort Laramie about six
or seven years ago, just after I came into the mountains.
I didn't know you were a captive.'

She nodded slowly. She started to speak and words did
not come. She cleared her throat and tried again.

'I … have not spoke … English for a long time. I
remember you vague, Charlie Webb. Are you planning to
take the boy back to his people?'

'Yes, Sara,' Charlie said softly. 'And you, too, now that
I know you are here.' He hesitated. There were times
when white women chose to remain with their Indian
husbands, being treated better by them than their
former white husbands. 'That is, if you want to come.'

She trembled again. It was the first time she felt she
might actually escape from the village. She had been
with the Utes three years, and before that with the
Navajos.

She hesitated. Did she wish to put her life in the hands
of a person she had only known slightly, in fact only knew
about him? Her life was safe here, there was no fighting
or trading between tribes at this time. The old chief was
reasonably good to her, so long as she was obedient to his
needs. But … out yonder … out there was her *real* world.
Maybe she might find her way back to Indiana where she
had originally come from with her husband. A firmness
entered her mind. It was worth a chance. If this man,
whom she remembered as being a mountain man, could
free her, then she must take the chance.

'Yes,' she whispered hoarsely. 'I will go with you. How can I help you with the boy? He is here. His name is Billy.'

Charlie sighed. He had found the boy. Now, his work really began. To escape the village, evade their searching bands that surely would spread out, seeking them, this would take all his energies and mountain knowledge.

'Here is what I want you to do, Sara.' He outlined a simple plan for her to get Billy to the trees where he was hiding. With the village caught up in the heavy work of preparing the meat, hides and other parts of the buffalo for movement back to the main village compound, their attention would be occupied. But stealth must be used to get away from the village without detection for several hours, at least. Webb was certain that eventually the Indian trackers would find their signs of passage, no matter how careful he was to hide their tracks.

Sara agreed to his plan, and with heart beating heavily in her chest, she entered the women's grounds, taking care of her personal needs. She left the grounds and moved across the village in the quickly darkening gloom. Walking around the perimeter of the camp, she approached the roped-off corrals where the animals were herded. The larger boys had charge of this chore, and were always near by. She stood and watched for a few minutes until she saw Billy Harris. She moved slowly and unobtrusively around to where he was in a shadow of trees, but close enough for him to hear her voice. At the moment there was no other boys near him.

'Leaping Deer,' she called softly, using his Indian name. 'Leaping Deer, I wish to speak with you. Can you take a moment to talk with me?'

His quick eye found her in the shadows and he came slowly toward her, still carrying a lariat he was braiding.

'Who are you' he answered. 'What do you want?'

He was close now, standing and looking up at her. She moved a step closer to him and whispered in English.

'I am white, like you,' she told him. He stiffened, his eyes narrowing.

'You speak real words,' he said haltingly, also in English. It had been several months since he had attempted to speak in his own tongue. 'What do you want?'

She was close to him now and bent so her face was close to his. 'Billy, there is a man out there in the darkness, who has come to help us escape from the village. He will take us back to Denver, where your uncle and aunt wait for you. They sent him to look for you.'

Suddenly he believed her. He drew a deep breath. 'What do you want me to do?'

She whispered, speaking haltingly in English. 'You go to the men's place, get back under the trees where none can see you. Then circle around the camp to that large pine tree you see there.' She pointed with her chin to the towering tree, whose height pushed it above all others about it. 'When you get there, a man will speak to you. It will be Charlie Webb. He is a good man, he is a mountain man, and as wise as any Indian. He was sent by your aunt and uncle to find you. Do what he says and you will be all right.'

'What about you?' he asked.

She smiled and touched his shoulder as she rose. 'I will be coming from the women's place and will join you.'

She vanished into the darkness of the night, moving toward the lights where the women were working on the carcasses of buffalo brought in that day. She knelt beside a friend and engaged her in conversation, applying herself to the humble task of carving joints of steaming flesh from the bodies of the animals.

Billy did as the woman had told him. He wandered into the place of the men, took care of himself, and then, keeping back in the forest edge, away from the light of the encampment, he moved slowly through the under-brush toward the large pine she had indicated.

It seemed to his eager mind to take hours, but in a short while he was at the tree. He stared at it, wondering if the white man hiding there could see him.

A huge, dark figure stepped around the bole of the tree and came toward him. He stepped back, suddenly deeply frightened and drew his breath as though to yell.

A big hand clasped itself across his mouth and he was pulled tightly against a huge body. A hoarse voice whispered in his ear.

'Billy! Don't be scared! I'm here to take you home. Don't make any noise. We'll be out of here in a minute. Just be quiet and come over here behind the tree where we won't be seen.'

Slowly Billy relaxed and nodded. The hand was removed and placed on his shoulder, led him back into the deeper shadows of the tree.

There was a slight crackling of a twig beneath a foot and the figure of the woman appeared against the skyline. Then she stood beside them.

Charlie Webb crept to the edge of the woods and knelt there for a long minute, watching and listening. Apparently the movement of the two people toward this spot had not been detected. He came back to them, moving silently through the underbrush.

'It's all right,' he whispered to them. 'It's time to go.'

TEN

Lightning Head spent much of his day overseeing the selection and final kill of the buffalo. They were not out this time for the sport of seeing how many of the animals they might slaughter. There was no chasing and firing from horseback. There was a methodical search and wary approach from the ground, the choosing of the right animal and the right spot for the arrow to lodge and drive deeply into the heart and lungs of the beast. There was no charging at a challenging bull and counting coup at a good slap on its rump or nose. Winter was nearing and this was the only time they had to bring in the needed meat and hides, before the snows fell and became deep and impassable.

Having bathed and changed to clean pants and over-shirt, the war chief approached an area where the butchering was still going on, even though darkness had fallen. He glanced around and seeing his wife, Bright Willow, walked over and touched her on the shoulder. She ceased her work at splitting a section of ribs for wrapping and rose to her feet.

'Greeting, my husband,' she said softly. 'May I get your evening meal prepared, my husband?'

He nodded to her and looking about, noted that Billy Harris was not among the boys playing around the village camp-fire.

'I do not see Leaping Deer. Is he with the ponies yet?' Bright Willow looked up at him and then glanced about. Not seeing Billy, she rose and turned slowly, observing the other boys but not seeing Billy.

'He was with the others not long ago. He must have wandered off. Maybe to the men's place.'

He looked around more and then decided to go to the pony corrals and see if the white boy was on duty there. 'I will be back for our meal in a few minutes. I will see you at our tepee. If Leaping Deer is not there after we eat, I will go look for him.'

The meal finished, Billy Harris had not appeared at their family tepee for his meal. This was unusual, for Bright Willow knew that the boy had a vigorous appetite. Lightning Head rose from their meal.

'I will go look for the boy,' he told her and left the lodge.

The tall, stoic war chief moved about the village, looking for the white boy. He stopped one lad and questioned him, but he had not seen Billy since it became dark.

Lightning Head went to the men's place. Coming from there was another brave and the war chief questioned him.

'The white boy is not here at the men's place,' he was told. 'I haven't seen him.'

A man of the forests, as well as war chief, the Indian turned and swept his eyes around the edges of the encampment, narrowing to focus into darkened spaces. As his gaze reached the large tree standing approximately between the places of the men and women, he

started and became absolutely still. The slender shape of
a woman was entering the forest edge, going into the
shadows of the large pine. There was no reason for her
to go into that area. The women's place was several yards
away. He watched as she disappeared into the darkness of
the forest.

Moving silently and quickly, he went in among the
bushes and smaller trees and made his way toward the
large pine. He paused and listened and heard the murmur
of voices. Moving silently and quickly, he approached the
tree.

'We must get away from here,' Webb whispered
hoarsely to Sara Wilcox and Billy. 'You will be missed
before long and they will start a search for you.'

Webb had turned to lead the way from the tree when
the bushes rustled near them. He paused. As he did so
Lightning Head launched himself from the darkness and
his strong, agile body slammed against the mountain
man, staggering him backward into small trees and brush
about the base of the tree. As he struggled to right
himself, the Indian seized him about the head and neck
and bracing himself, attempted to wrestle Webb to the
ground. But suddenly he realized that the man he was
attacking was huge, larger and heavier than he. Webb
growled and seizing the Indian by an arm slammed him
to the ground and, kneeling on his chest, struck him with
rights and lefts in the face and neck.

Sara Wilcox drew Billy around the tree, away from the
struggle of the two men. 'If Webb is killed by Lightning
Head,' she whispered, 'we will run deeper into the forest.
Perhaps we can escape by ourselves.' Billy shivered and
pressed closer to her. He could hear the heavy breathing
and thrashing of Webb and the war chief, as they each
struggled for mastery.

The Indian was strong and, withstanding Webb's blows, not directly reaching vital spots, he suddenly squirmed from beneath Webb's weight and, as he fell away, savagely kicked the mountain man in the chest and side. Lightning Head rolled away from the huge white man, seized him about the head and threw himself backwards, squeezing Webb's throat with steel-like fingers. Webb clawed at the tightening stranglehold of the Indian and, drawing back, his tremendous strength forcing the Indian to rise with him, he slammed both hands against the Ute war chief's ears. The unexpected pain in his ears and head caused the Indian to gasp and momentarily release his hold.

Taking advantage of the brief moment, Webb doubled his fists together and, with all his strength, clubbed the Indian in the face. Lightning Head fell backwards, his lips and nose smashed and spraying blood. Grunting with the effort, Webb struck again and the Indian went limp beneath him, unconscious from the blows.

Gasping for breath, Webb fell back and lay gathering his strength. The woman and Billy slipped around the tree, and Sara knelt beside him. Using a soft cloth she wiped his face of sweat and blood.

'Are you hurt badly?' she asked softly. He shook his head.

'No. Just winded. The blood on my face is from his nose and mouth.' He rose and sat looking over at the inert form of the Indian. 'There is one strong Indian,' he muttered. He struggled to his feet. He eyed the form of the Indian thoughtfully.

'Are you going to kill him?' Billy whispered hoarsely. Sara looked at Webb, awaiting his answer.

Webb shook his head. 'No. He was just defending his village. You can't fault any man for fighting for what he believes in, especially if it involves his family or home. No, we'll tie him so he won't get loose for a few hours and maybe by then we'll be far enough away so they won't catch up with us until we hit civilization.'

He drew his knife and, kneeling, cut strips from the Indian's blouse. He proceeded to bind the Indian's ankles and, with a longer strip, anchored them to a tree. With another strip of the finely cured leather he bound the war chief's arms tightly, rolling the body over and knotting the bonds with the hands behind. This done, he cut a broader strip of the blouse and forced a piece of branch between his teeth, and bound it, gagging him, securing the bond firmly back of his head. With another long strip of the leather, he tied one end about the Indian's throat, and secured it about the bole of another smaller tree. His task completed, he rose and looked at Sara.

'He is strong. He will awaken in an hour or two. It will take him some time to get loose, but he will. But, by that time, we will have found our horses, and be away from here.'

'You have horses?' asked Billy, his interest drawn suddenly away from the scene.

Webb nodded. 'One for you and Sara,. I didn't know she was here or I would have brought one for her.'

Billy grinned. 'I can ride double, don't worry.'

Webb looked about. He listened intently, but could hear nothing beyond the murmur of the village busily finishing up their butchering of the day's catch of buffalo. He crept to the edge of the bushes and squatted, silently and keenly watching and listening. Apparently his battle with the Indian had not drawn any attention. However, he knew that Lightning Head would eventually regain his senses and free himself from his bonds. They had at least two, perhaps three hours before any alarm was raised.

He returned to the woman and Billy. 'It seems to be quiet at the moment. The Indian has apparently not been missed, nor your absence noticed.'

'Good!' said Billy Harris. 'Let's get outta here!'

ELEVEN

Laff Brock, the second in command of the gang headed by Roman McClure, was restless and bored. They had built a shed for the horses, gathered hay from the nearby meadows, raised some fencing so the animals would not stray. Together they had build a rickety two-room shack from timber nearby, and some planks and slabs of wood that had not burned when the Indians had killed Walt Harris and his wife and carried away their son. Now, there was nothing for them to do but wait for the spring, lie low and keep away from the law.

'Be patient,' McClure told them. 'Practice your shooting, ride out and get fresh meat. There's deer close by and I saw some stray beef down in the brakes by the creek. Come spring, we'll make a quick visit to that bank in Denver, and we'll all share real *dinero*.'

This was all fine for Brock, but finally, after several dust-ups with members of the gang, he decided to visit the saloons in Denver, find some female companionship and generally tear loose for a while from the humdrum of the outback where they were all dreading the thought of the winter to come.

Without informing McClure or any of the other

members of the gang, he quietly saddled his horse one noon and rode out, heading across the mountains for Denver and its promise of momentary pleasure.

Clarence Harris was at his usual table in the saloon, going over some bills with the barkeep, when Brock pushed through the batwing doors and strode purposefully up to the bar. He pounded on the wood before the barkeep could leave the table and appear to serve him.

'Whiskey,' he snarled at the barkeep. 'An' none of that hogwash you usually serve. I want a bottle of your best.'

Clarence watched and listened from the table. He smelled trouble. He recognized Brock and was surprised to see him without his boss nearby. There was only a small crowd in the bar at the time, the after supper regulars not having appeared yet.

Tim Holland, the barkeep, eyed his customer carefully. He recognized trouble and wondered why the man was so disturbed. He reached under the bar and brought up a quart of rye. 'This is good Pennsylvania rye. Just in. How about a jigger of this?'

'Rye? That's fer womenfolks at parties and dandiprats that don't know their whiskey. I want Kentucky bourbon, or St Louis redeye.' Brock turned to set his back against the bar. 'I want a drink that will warm the belly, fire up the brain, an' give a twist of the devil's tail at the same time.'

A cowhand from a ranch near Denver, in for the evening, as was Brock, laughed at him. 'Yore in the wrong place, mister. There's no fancy stuff here. It's skull-pop, an' that's the best you will get.'

Brock turned slowly and eyed the cowhand. The cowboy stared back at him and then grinned a sly grin. Brock looked at the barkeep. 'Jist give me a bottle of whatever you sell in this place, an' I'll see whether it's worth a quarter a shot.'

Clarence rose from his chair and started to go to the bar, then he paused. The cowhand had pushed back his chair and was grinning at Brock.

'You come in here like you was a ring-tailed daddy coon from the mountains. Iffen you don't like the liquor sold here, then shut your yap an' stop makin' noises. Maybe just mosey off to some other waterin'-hole.'

Brock whirled on the man, snarling, his hand swept down and came up holding his sixgun. Suddenly the grin was gone from the face of the cowboy. He sat back down in the chair and put his hands up.

'Aw, come on, friend. I was just joshin'. Go on an' pour your drink. In fact, I'll buy.'

Tim Holland reached over, filled a shot glass and pushed it toward Brock. 'There's your drink, friend. Just pay ol' Buck there no mind. He's always spoutin' off about something and mostly it's none of his business.'

Brock shook his head. 'No man tells me what to do. I'm gonna put my iron back in the leather.' He leveled a finger at the one who had seemingly challenged him. 'I'll count three, an' if you ain't outta that chair when I get to three, I'll shoot you where you set.'

'One!' Brock spread his legs in a straddled position balancing himself, his hand hovering over his now sheathed sixgun.

The cowhand, his face suddenly blanched, gulped. 'Now, look a-here, mister. I didn't mean nothin'—'

'Two!' Brock stepped away from the bar, his body tense, his right hand quivering over the butt of his sixgun.

'What's going on here?' The batwing doors of the saloon parted and Henry Culpepper, the town marshal, stepped in and paused, taking in the tableau.

'None of your concern, lawman, jist stay outta this,' Brock snarled at the marshal. 'I'll get around to you later.'

'You're outta line, mister. Now, back off and we'll get to the bottom of this. There'll be no gunplay in my town.'

Brock turned his head, looked at the marshal. He drew a deep breath, and then tensed as a shotgun was poked against his kidneys.

'Loosen up, mister,' Tim Holland said softly, but with steel in his tones. 'Like the marshal just said, there'll be no gunplay here, not in town, nor in my saloon.'

The marshal looked at him levelly and nodded. 'Do as he says. And take your hand away from that sixgun. Move away from the bar and sit down at that table there. We'll talk.'

Again Brock tensed and then his eyes blinked. He had not seen the marshal's hand move, but there was a revolver cocked and the bore held steadily on him. Slowly he relaxed and spread his hands from his sides.

'I ain't done nothin', lawman. You ain't got nothing against me.'

Marshal Culpepper nodded and pointed the gun at the table nearest Brock. 'Not yet you ain't. Now, set.' Brock snorted and moved over. He sat down, noisily slamming himself into a chair and slapping his hands on the table. The marshal looked over at Clarence Harris.

'Has he caused any trouble, I don't know about?'

Clarence shook his head. 'No. You got here just in time. But he's not welcome in my place of business, unless he behaves himself.'

Brock snorted again and cursed. 'What kind of a penny-anti town is this? I jist come in to get a drink an' here I have the law jawin' at me.'

Marshal Culpepper sat across the table from Brock. 'We have very little trouble in Denver, but mostly it's from too much cheap whiskey at the wrong time. Now, my advice to you is to get your drink, and move on. Where's your headquarters, anyway?'

Brock eyed him sullenly. 'You ain't my boss. Me an' some fellows are camped a few miles from here. I jist come in to stretch my legs a bit and get me a drink. I don't mean no trouble. But it seems to follow me around.'

The marshal nodded. 'Seems so. Where are you camped?'

Brock hesitated and then he shrugged. 'I guess it's no secret. Anyone ridin' past would know. We come in lookin' for some land. The boss, Roman McClure, asked around and was told of a place about thirty miles from here where Injuns had killed. There's two graves there. So we threw up a shack and are waitin' until the boss decides whether to bring his herd and crew from Texas.'

Clarence Harris heard the man's explanation. He rose from his table, came over and pulled out another chair, joining them. He looked at Brock.

'Was there a chimney standing? An' a shed or two that still had some planks that had not burned?'

Brock nodded. 'Yup. We just threw up a shanty against the fireplace an' another shed for the hosses.'

Clarence looked at the marshal. 'Henry, that sounds like my brother's place. It's on a high mesa overlooking some good grasslands and well watered. The two graves would be that of my brother and his wife, Mary. Me and some other men went out there, and buried them.'

He faced Brock. 'Tell your boss, McClure, that the place is not for sale, under any circumstances. He can come in and discuss it with me. As for your camping there for a while, I guess it's all right. But, by my brother's Will, I am the owner of the ranch.'

Brock sneered at the saloon owner. 'I reckon the boss will talk to you about it. But, if he likes the place, I suspect he'll stay. After all, possession is said to be nine-tenths of the law.' He pushed back his chair. 'I'll go find myself another bar where I'm welcome. This one has turned real unfriendly.' He rose and glared at the marshal. 'An' don't be followin' me around. It's still a free country.'

Three days after Brock's informing him that McClure might declare ownership of his brother's ranch, by the simple right of possession, Clarence Harris saddled his horse and, with provisions for several days away, left Denver. The marshal knew his destination, and his wife, but he had told no one else. To his bartender, Tim Holland, he simply said he would be away several days on business.

On a clear morning, three days later, he rode across the mesa, crossed the creek and headed up the long slope to where he could see the chimney thrusting upward. He recalled helping his brother dig out the rocks and plane them, shaping them and stone on stone, erecting the chimney.

He drew up in the space before the cabin and called out. 'Hello, the house. Anyone home?'

A man appeared from the shed where he could see a horse tethered. The man held a horseshoe in his hand and a hammer. About his waist, however, was belted a sixgun. He stopped at the corner of the shabbily built cabin and stared at Clarence.

'Who wants to know?'

At the sound of his voice, Brock appeared from the back of the cabin.

'What do you want, barkeeper? There ain't no liquor for you hereabouts.'

Clarence leaned on his saddle horn, his eyes locked on Brock's face. 'Most times when a neighbor comes callin',' he said, 'he's invited down for at least a drink of water, and made welcome.'

Roman McClure opened the cabin door and stepped out on hardpan of the now weed-grown yard. He was smoking a cigar and stared over at Harris.

'What are you doing here? No one invited you to visit.'

Clarence had expected such a welcome. 'Your foreman, Brock, indicated the other evening at my place in Denver that you might be planning on putting down permanent residence here. I thought I'd talk with you about it.'

'What's to say? We're here, and if I like the place, I'll send for my herd later and make this my headquarters.'

Clarence shook his head. 'McClure, this is my property, my ranch. My brother's body and that of his wife lie there.' He pointed to the spot where the graves were. 'He willed it to me and I'm holding it until his son can be found and then I'll work it in trust for him until he's old enough to take it over himself. It's not for sale. I'd suggest you look further for a place to settle in. Not on my property.'

McClure tapped ash from his cigar and drawing on it deeply, he exhaled the smoke, all the time listening to Clarence.

'It'll take more than you to get me out of here, now that I've settled in for the winter,' McClure said roughly. 'If you want to make a war out of this, then we'll be ready. Now, Brock, turn the man around and point him back the way he came.'

Brock grinned and spat. 'Sure thing, boss.' He gestured to two of the men now standing and watching at the shed. 'Come over here, boys. The gentleman needs a little lesson in manners.' McClure stared at Clarence for a moment, then turning his back he entered the cabin and shut the door.

Brock grabbed Clarence's leg and before Harris knew what was happening the big man had yanked him from the saddle. He landed heavily on his back on the ground, the breath jarred out of him. He twisted and attempted to rise, when Brock kicked him in the side. Clarence groaned and fell back.

'Get him on his feet,' Brock growled at the two men. They grabbed Clarence on either side and lifted him from the ground, holding him between them. Brock stepped in front of him. 'This is a lesson for you to remember. What McClure wants, he gets. And we're here to help him. Understand?'

With that he reared back and then powered his fist into the saloon-keeper's stomach. Clarence gasped for breath and fell to his knees, clasping his belly. Brock made a motion and the men lifted him again and held him between them.

'This is to remember not to stick your nose in something that ain't none of your business.' With that he struck Clarence in the face, smashing his nose and mouth. The blood poured from his bruised nose and he staggered weakly as the two men released him and stepped away.

'Put him on his hoss and head him outta here. The hoss should be able to find his way home, if he's too addled to guide him.'

The two men lifted Clarence into the saddle and put the reins in his hands. 'Now, get out of here,' one of them said gruffly. 'An' I'd advise you not to come back.'

Weakly, Clarence raised the reins and gigged the horse gently in the flanks. He left the clearing, riding down the slope and onto the thin trail that led over the mountains to Denver.

He was scarcely conscious enough to realize the horse was going the right way. 'If I don't fall off, I just might make it,' he thought. That was the last thing he remembered.

TWELVE

Three forms moved swiftly through the darkness of the forest. There was no moon and only starlight penetrated the darkness dimly, lighting their way.

Charlie Webb, however, had scouted the area thoroughly. He knew every coulee, every cul-de-sac, every ridge and swale. He led the woman and boy, cautioning each to step carefully, make as little noise as possible.

'The horses are about three miles from here. We'll find the horses and, with any luck, will be away from here by daylight.' They had paused briefly for breath. He listened carefully, retracing their way until he could not hear their deep breathing, made so by their swift passage over, for them, unknown ground. He could hear no pursuit.

In a few minutes they were on their way again. Each of them had brought a small bundle of possessions, including a blanket. These they strapped on their backs, feeling the weight only briefly as they walked silently and swiftly through the night.

Finally, Webb brought them to a pause. 'The horses are over the next rise, in a small meadow. We will get them and be on our way. We have been lucky so far.'

After a short pause, he led out and in a few minutes they topped the rise and he motioned for them to stay low among some brush, while he went into the meadow to locate the animals.

Webb moved about the perimeter of the small grassed cove, listening for any sounds of the horses, a snuffle, teeth clipping at a bunch of grass. But he heard nothing. Moving cautiously, he entered the meadow and crouching, swept the place slowly with intent gaze. The horses were gone! Had they been driven off by someone who'd found them? Had they been discovered by Indians? For long minutes he searched and listened.

Moving on he located grass pressed down into the loam where one of them had slept. Nearby he found a pile of manure. He now moved swiftly, covering the small meadow in a short while. Finally he made his way back to the woman and the boy.

'Either the horses have strayed, or someone has found them and driven them away.' He looked at them silently for a moment and then shrugged. 'We're on our own feet, my friends. And it is going to be a long walk to Denver.'

'But you know the way, don't you?' whispered Billy. 'You know these trails.'

Webb nodded in the darkness. 'Yes, I know the way. But that is not the only problem. The Indians know, by now, that you are gone. They will find our tracks and follow. By mid-morning they will be here in this meadow and read the signs as have I. So,' he paused and looked at them. 'If we are careful, travel most of the time by night, we will make it. It is going to take time and we'll probably still be out here when the first snows come. But we will take it one day at a time. Now,' he straightened and shrugged his bundle of possessions into a more

comfortable position, 'let's get some distance behind us
before daylight comes and White Bear's trackers are after
us.'

Lightning Head was furious. He awakened to find those
who had bound him gone, and he was tied firmly with
strips of his own clothing. He struggled and, finally,
worked off the gag Webb had placed in his mouth. He
worked silently and steadily at his bound feet and arms,
but the tethers, stretching him between two trees finally
caused him to cease his struggles and think.

Just where was he? He lifted his head and looked
about. It was dawn and the shadows of the night were
leaving. He recalled the large tree at the edge of the
women's place, and knew his location. He realized what
he must do. It shamed him to think that he, the war
chief, had been so bested by a woman and a boy, with
some stranger he had not recognized in the dark.

At last he heard voices in the distance. He called out
several times, all the while struggling with his bonds. But
they would not loosen. He called again and heard footsteps. A woman appeared through the bushes and
approached him cautiously. When she saw the war chief,
she turned and started to run, but then, recognizing
him, hurried to his side.

The council sat in a circle around the fire. Chief White
Bear sat with his back to the opening of his tepee. Sub-
chiefs sat silently, waiting for him to open the subject of
the call. Most of them were aware of what was to be
discussed, for the story of the woman finding Lightning
Head bound in the forest, and the two white captives
gone, had flowed through the village.

Lightning Head had warned the woman who had

released him that she should not say anything about what she had done. But the secret was shared with a close friend, and a secret, once disclosed, soon becomes general knowledge.

Lightning Head had gone to the chief and related the incident, telling the chief he would leave immediately and find the culprit and bring the woman and the boy back to the village. But the old chief disagreed.

'This is a matter for the council,' he said. 'We will talk after the evening meal and see what is best to do.' Lightning Head knew it was useless to argue with the old chief, so he fretted and fumed through the day, staying away from usual companions, and working silently at his tepee. Having heard the story as it made its rounds, Bright Willow moved silently about her duties, wondering if she would ever see the boy, Leaping Deer, again. She had become attached to the white boy, and felt sorrow that he would probably no longer be part of her life. She did not, however, relate her thoughts and feelings to her husband, but honored his desire for silence.

White Bear cleared his throat at last. He raised his eyes, pausing briefly as he passed each face. 'Our war chief has discovered that the white woman, who was my personal slave, and the white boy, Leaping Deer, have escaped. They did not escape on their own, but were helped by a white man. They have been gone since dark last night. There was no moon, so it was easy to slip away and not be seen.'

Members of the council grunted and muttered among themselves. After a minute or two, the chief continued:

'Lightning Head has asked that he and at least two other braves track them and bring them back. It is my thinking that it is more important to finish our gathering of the buffalo before the winter moons come bringing great winds and much snow and cold. White slaves can be captured or traded from the Navajo or Apache or other tribes.' He fell silent and looked around the circle. After a period of silence, Lightning Head spoke.

'White Bear is wise and I bow to his wisdom. The meat is more important than any white eyes. But the village is shamed when a woman and a mere boy can escape and no one tries to bring them back. I will go by myself and find them and kill the one helping them, whoever it might be.'

Others spoke, some siding with the chief, some with Lightning Head. Two volunteered to go with him to find the slaves and return them. The old chief listened to all. Finally, when everyone had spoken and fell silent, he spoke again.

'I have listened to you. I will now say what I feel is the best action for all, for the village. Three men, and that means three hands, are gone that would help with the meat gathering. It must be done in half a moon. Then we will return to our lodges. At that time, we will take up the problem of recapturing the white woman and the boy, and punishing whoever enticed them away. After all,' he continued after a slight pause, 'she was my slave.'

There was no further discussion concerning the loss of the two captives. To the majority of the council the harvesting of the winter's sustenance from the buffalo was far more important than spending time tracking down and retaking two white slaves. The words had been spoken, the council had decided. It was done.

Apparently all of the council, with the exception of one or two of Lightning Head's close friends, agreed on the subject. Lightning Head, however, returned to his tepee. He told Bright Willow he was going to be gone for a few

days, and prepared to follow and track down the captives
and their benefactor. He restrung his war bow, chose his
best arrows, sharpened his knife and, after considera-
tion, decided not to take the rifle he owned, one of only
a half-dozen in the village. What needed to be done
would be accomplished with the weapons he knew best.

There are times when the powers controlling the
elements bring unexpected surprises. When Webb rolled
from his blankets the morning after their escape from
the village, there was six inches of early snow fallen, and
more drifting down in feathery profusion. He grinned to
himself. This would take care of covering their tracks
from anyone trying to follow them. This was not
expected, it was early for snow, at these heights. But here
it was and they were at least ten days ahead of any trackers. He aroused Sara and Billy and after a meager breakfast from their slim supply of food, they set out again,
following a direction Webb set, reaching deeply into his
memory of an earlier trip through this section of mountains beyond Denver. They had a long way to go and,
while the snow slowed their walking, it hid the direction
of their passage, at least while the snow lasted. This early
in the season the sun could very well melt the early snowfall, and a seasoned tracker, such as most villages had,
could soon pick up their signs.

'We will cover as much ground as possible,' he told
them, 'because the village will have scouts out as soon as
possible.'

In the village, Lightning Head fumed and paced. Every
hour he waited until he might locate signs of their escape
gave them that same amount of time to put more miles
between them and the village. Whatever signs they might

leave would dim with the elements as the days passed.

Now the early snow covered their tracks, and he could only pace in frustration.

THIRTEEN

Two hunters came into Denver, leading a horse with an inert body draped across the saddle. They inquired for a doctor and were directed to his home and place of business. The doctor, seeing the body draped over the saddle when he answered their knock, simply opened the door wider and directed them to bring the body into his office, where he watched as they placed it on the cot in the office.

He bent over the body and turned the face up. He stepped back in surprise. 'Where did you find him?' he asked one of the hunters.

'Just outside the town. His hoss hadn't wandered off, so we hung him across the saddle and brung him to you.'

'Did you know who you were bringing in?' asked the doctor, again stepping to the side of the limp, unconscious body on the cot.

'Nope,' they both shook their heads. 'Cain't say as we do. But we didn't get a right good look at his face, clobbered up as bad as it is.'

'He's the owner of the saloon and partner in the mercantile here in town,' the doctor informed them.

'His name is Clarence Harris.' He looked at the hunters. 'You fellows are strangers in town, but I know Clarence's wife would like to know about him. It would be right neighborly if you went to their home and told her he was here.'

One of the hunters nodded. 'We kin do that, Doc. Do you think he'll be all right?'

The doctor was busy searching Clarence's body for broken bones, knife wounds, or other causes of his being in such bad shape. 'Oh, I reckon he'll live,' he said. 'But someone surely pounded him up good. I think he's got some broken ribs, and he may be banged up some inside. His belly is turning black, as it is.'

With the doctor's directions, the two men left, going to the Harris home and informing his wife that her husband had been hurt and was in the doctor's office.

'Let's go to that saloon the sawbones mentioned, and sample some of Harris's red eye,' one suggested. 'I wouldn't want to be him when he wakes up and starts movin' around. Broke ribs kin smart purty much until they heal.'

Samantha Harris was at the doctor's office almost before the two men found the saloon and were leaning against the bar, feet propped up on the foot-rail.

The doctor met Samantha at the door. 'Is he bad hurt?' she asked breathlessly, her face pale with anxiety.

'Come on in, Samantha.' He held the door open for her. 'He's been beaten within an inch of his life, as I see it. Someone or some persons have given him a terrible going over.'

'Oh … my God … is he …?'

The doctor patted her shoulder. 'I'm awkward with my words, I guess, Samantha. He's been badly mauled, but he'll live. In fact, he'll be up and about in a day or two, although aching a bunch, what with three broken ribs and a bruised belly.'

She went to her husband and leaned over to kiss his forehead. 'Thank God, it's no worse,' she murmured. 'Do what you can for him, Doctor.'

Charlie Webb moved on through the snowy day. He knew by the lessening of the falling snow that it soon would ease and that the accumulation would soon melt with tomorrow's sun. Although it was heavy going, he pushed Sara and Billy to their limits, putting as much distance as possible between them and the village.

It was growing dark when the snow finally ceased falling and a weak sun shone briefly before it sank behind the lift of the mountains they were on. He paused at a small stream and removed the pack from his shoulders.

'We'll rest for an hour and then go on until it's full dark. There is a cave not far from here. We'll use it, build a fire and have a hot meal.'

They followed his actions and dropped their bundles. Webb saw the strain of fatigue on their faces and realized they were nearing the end of their endurance. They must rest.

He stooped to lift his pack when there was a snuffle and then a deep growl. He whirled about and he tensed, his eyes widening. Standing on the edge of the bank of the stream from which Webb was preparing to drink, was a bear. Huge, dark, with silvery fur about the throat and head, he realized it was a mountain grizzly. He had seen them at a distance, and made certain he gave the animal's turf plenty of room. There was no way he would tempt the charge of such an animal. But here one was, across the small stream of water, the great head moving back and forth as it took his scent, the weak eyes unable to know exactly where he was. But any move, any sudden start, would tell it where he stood and undoubtedly bring a charge.

He heard Sara gasp back of him. 'Shhh,' he breathed. 'Get Billy up the bank and behind them trees. If it charges, climb any tree and stay there until it leaves, or I come to get you. Now! Move!'

Holding Billy's hand tightly, she moved back slowly, stepping silently on leaves and grass, knowing that any noise would bring the animal's attention more directly upon them.

The bear had located Webb's position. It rose on hind feet, and Webb saw that it was a male. Late in the autumn, the mating season was long gone, and he was now foraging, eating and building up fat upon which his body would feed during hibernation.

Rearing, the animal was six and a half feet or more in height. I'm six feet six, thought Webb, and that animal tops me by inches. The animal growled and then suddenly roared with an angry bellow, dropping to its feet and snapping huge jaws. In another second the bear charged across the small stream of water, sending spray in every direction, some of it splattering Webb. Eight hundred pounds or more of angry grizzly charged across the stream, its eyes red with anger at its turf being invaded by a strangely scented animal.

Sara and Billy, trembling with fear, watched the horrible animal as it lurched into the water and splashed its way across the stream, eyes fastened upon Webb, who was slowly backing away.

Webb knew that death stared at him with rage-reddened eyes. He knew the grizzly was attacking him, not because he was human, or because he was merely another animal with whom to enter combat. He was declaring this his territory which a stranger had entered. Nature called for him to protect what was his, and this pushed him into the conflict. Webb backed away, smoothly, quickly, turning so the grizzly would not catch the scent of the other two humans, but place all his attention on Webb. Never try to outrun a grizzly, Webb had been told by older and more experienced mountain men. Keep moving slowly, or do as others had done, roll up into a tight ball and live through the mauling of the animal. Or, the thought ran through Webb's mind, pick a place on the animal's body and empty your sixgun into it.

This last thought had no sooner occurred to him than the animal arrived on Webb's side of the stream. As he lurched up the bank, the grizzly reared up on his hind feet. Seven feet tall at least, reasoned Webb. Without thought, his hand slashed down to his sixgun and brought it up firing. One after another the shots roared out in the narrow creek bed, the bullets finding a lodging in the massive, charging body. The bear hesitated momentarily and roared, shaking his head, with blood flying about him. At least one of the bullets had torn into a lung. But the bear still charged. Webb, having paused in his retreat almost stumbled as he moved back away from the staggering, roaring animal. He drew his knife, a Bowie blade, given him by a dying mountain man. 'Keep it keen,' he was advised. 'It may one day be the difference between life and death for you'. How true the old mountain man's words were. Here he was, facing a mountain of frenzied bear, moving in on him.

The bear roared again and staggered. The bullets emptied into his body were taking effect, but there was still an indescribable danger in the animal; it was still capable of ultimate destruction. Webb held his knife poised, and with a sudden lurch of determination, fired by unreasoned sudden anger at being in such a position, he closed in on the animal and felt the huge arms enfold him, squeezing him breathless. At the same time he drove the blade deeply into the armpit, through the soft, unguarded flesh, the keen point digging into the massive heart.

Webb's breath was leaving him. The claws of the giant paw were ripping the clothes from his back, and he felt the dig of the sharp claws ripping into his flesh. He was weakening; fighting against the crushing strength of the beast's forearms, he continued to gouge with the knife, feeling it moving, ripping inside the body, squeezing the life from it

Suddenly the bear shivered, the giant body quaked. The bear roared and released Webb from its grasp. Rearing to its full height again, shaking the massive head and roaring, the bear fell back, the giant body continuing to quake and shiver, then, with a final grunt, it was dead.

In falling, one of the bear's paws had pulled Webb against the beast's side, holding him close in a suffocating embrace. He groaned and Sara, emerging from her hiding place, heard him. She approached cautiously and, assuming that the animal was dead, ran to Webb's side, with Billy, white-faced with fright, at her heels.

'Charlie!' she called. 'Charlie, can you hear me.' Webb groaned again and she saw him move beneath the giant paw of the bear. Bending over the animal, she tugged at the arm and paw holding Webb in a final embrace. Grunting, she put both hands and arms into the job, and slowly lifted the great limb from about its intended victim. As Webb's body emerged, she gasped.

His back was one mass of torn flesh, skin ripped away, muscle-fibres exposed.

'Billy! Come help me pull him away from the bear,' she ordered, and with both of them pulling and tugging, they separated the man's body from the stiffening hold of the dead grizzly.

'Charlie, can you hear me?'

Webb grunted and attempted to move. At the slightest stir of muscles, he yelled in pain.

'Charlie. Listen to me. You're hurt real bad. We gotta get out of here. Now, tell me where is that cave you told us about. We gotta get out of the weather.'

Webb opened an eye, blinked and then opened both. 'God, I hurt. Where are we?'

'We're near that cave you mentioned. Direct me, and I'll get you on your feet and take you there. It's going to snow again and we have to get inside somewhere, with you so hurt.'

'Help me to my feet.' he whispered hoarsely, his face twisted in pain. He sat up and gritted his teeth. Sara replaced as much as she could of the ripped coat he was wearing, grimacing as she covered the angry wounds in his back. With her help he rose, groaning in torture of ripped flesh and bruised body. On his feet he swayed and then, looking around with pain-squinted eyes, studied the area where they were, searching the direction he had been leading them.

'There, about a mile, maybe a little more. It's pretty hard to see, but I'll know when we are there.' He looked about. 'Billy, find my rifle, will you? And my knife,' he said to Sara, 'get my knife out of the bear.'

'I already found your rifle,' Billy told him, lifting the weapon for him to see. 'There's snow in the barrel, but I can get that out with a skinny twig of some kind.'

Sara shook her head. 'I tried to pry the knife outta its side, but it's buried so deep I can't budge it. We'll come back for it later.'

He grunted and tried to straighten, but the pain in his lacerated back brought him to a half-crouch, half-stance. 'Let's get movin',' he said. 'This new snow will cover our tracks and maybe hide the bear's body from any Indian hunter. We go this way.' He pointed up the stream, and over the lips of the defile where the bear had attacked.

It was a slow, painful procession that moved through the high meadows, painful for Webb, and difficult for Sara, supporting him best she could. It was full dark and Webb led them by the dim reflection of starlight off the snow. At last he stopped and straightened the best he could. 'See that boulder yonder?' he pointed up the slope they were on. Between two huge pines Sara could see the shoulders of a large boulder. From where she stood, she could not see any opening.

'The last time I was here, at least four years ago, I cut and piled brush against the opening. The hole is rather small, and we'll have to crawl on hands and knees to get in. But once inside it opens up on a large room. It has been used for centuries for just the same reason we are using it.'

He was walking straighter now, and went before them. Passing through some tangles of wild berry bushes and small trees, they came to the boulder. Dried branches and brush hid the opening, and the snow had covered the bushes. Unless one was aware of the cave being there, it would have been passed by.

Quickly Sara and Billy cleared the opening. Webb sank to his haunches in the snow, and watched them through pain-filled eyes. Once the hole was opened, Sara looked at Webb.

'Got any matches?' she asked. He nodded and stirring painfully searched a pocket in the large coat. He came up with a small tin of matches. She took them, and then searched among the dead branches that had covered the cave opening, found a larger limb which, when broken, gave her a club about four feet long. She took from her bosom a square of cloth and wound it about the head of the club, making a torch.

'I'll go in and see if there's no animals hibernating inside. If it's a bear, stand back. I'll come out of that hole like a storm.'

Webb stirred. 'Sara, let me do it. That's not a woman's work.'

She snorted, unladylike. 'What do you think I've been doin' for the last five years? Knittin' bootees?'

She knelt before the cave mouth and, sheltered from the wind, struck one of the sulphur matches from Webb's store, lighting the torch. The flame wavered, moving slowly through the material, then became firmer and gave her flame to go light her way into the cave. She glanced at Webb and smiled wryly, and, turning to Billy winked at him. She dropped to hands and knees and entered the cave.

In a few minutes she returned. Climbing to her feet she doused the burned-down torch and looked at Webb.

'It's clear and clean. An' apparently no animal has used it for some time. There's dry wood in there,' she told Billy. 'When we get in, gather up a pile of it and build a good fire, for it's purty damp. Now,' she reached down for her bundle, 'let's get out of this weather.'

It was a struggle for Webb, his back flaming with pain, to take himself through the cave mouth. His big body filled the entrance and he had to force himself along, scraping both sides of the hole. Sara had gone before him and, with another torch, lighted his way into the large room. Billy came in last with Webb's pack and the rifle.

Sara spread Webb's blankets on the cave floor, near where the fire would be built. When he laid himself upon them, he groaned and turned on his belly. A few minutes later Sara, checking on him, found him unconscious. His great strength had finally deserted him and he lay inert, vulnerable to whatever might happen.

FOURTEEN

Clarence Harris was in the office of the town marshal, Henry Culpepper. He was looking over a handful of flyers on wanted characters in the territories.

'I don't know that these characters will be in that bunch of pictures or not,' Henry told him as he settled in a chair beside the desk and began shuffling the well-worn flyers.

'These two characters that pounded on me just might be in here, or one other of their gang,' Clarence said. 'They are a scruffy-looking bunch except for the boss, McClure. He stood in the door and watched them thump me and pile me on my horse. He was kinda dandy in looks.'

He stared at a picture and started to lay it aside, when he hesitated and looked more closely at the face on the page. Bold letters beneath the picture read: WANTED FOR BANK ROBBERY. And a price of a thousand dollars was printed below the picture. The amount of reward was smudged and somewhat roughened by much handling and folding. He held it up to the light from the window and examined it carefully. He laid it down on the desk and put a blunt forefinger on it.

'That's McClure, all right. He's the leader of the bunch. It says here he's a wanted bank robber. I'd say the others about him are of the same ilk. So, Hank, we have a gang of bank robbers roostin' up out there at my brother's ranch. And you can guess what's on McClure's mind, can't you?'

The marshal picked up the flyer and studied it. 'If you say that's the man, then I take your word for it. I've never seen him, but he ain't in town that much.'

'But he's been in the bank,' Clarence pointed out. 'He talked to Will Martin about any places up for sale or lease around here. Now he's throwed up some shacks on my brother's property and says he is there to stay.'

The marshal laid the flyer down. 'You know my jurisdiction stops at the town limits here. But I can wire the sheriff's office and he can send some men over. I suspect that if McClure plans to rob the Denver bank, then he's waitin' for better weather. Maybe even spring. But I'll let the sheriff know, for sure.'

Charlie Webb was in bad shape. During the first night in the cave, Sara took the frying-pan from their supplies, and heated water from the nearby creek. She ripped off the major part of her underskirt and tore it into strips. She soaked these in hot water and laid them over the terrible scratches on Webb's back. At the touch of the cloth on his wounds he yelled in pain and then, gritting his teeth, he made no sound during the rest of the application.

Sara continued the application of hot water, all the time wishing she had some of the small bundles of healing herbs the old village shaman used for wounds, scrapes and bruises. But eight inches of snow covered all things, and she could not even gather those plants and leaves with which she was familiar. Grimly she continued with the poultices of hot water, hoping against hope it would hold off infection. She had been told by the village shaman that animal bites often brought poison in the blood, due to animals often eating spoiled meat of other animals already dead.

There was still food in Webb's pack. This she found and prepared for herself and Billy. One afternoon, when the fever seemed to have lessened and Webb was sleeping, she and Billy slipped away and made their way back to where the body of the huge bear was lying. Because of the freezing temperature, the body was stiffened and hard.

Working with Webb's knife, they managed to hack off a shoulder and, dragging it through the snow, made it back to the cave. There Sara laid the meat near the fire and when it had thawed, skinned it and sliced from it several layers of fat and muscle. Before long, the odor of cooking meat filled the cave, and Billy sat close, drooling, tending the skillet, turning the steaks of bear meat, so they would cook through and not burn. When finished they devoured the steaks with dripping fingers, as though they had never before enjoyed such eating. Once Billy glanced over at Sara, grinning, his face greasy, his mouth full. She winked at him and smiled. It had been a long time since either of them had enjoyed the full taste of meat.

After three days, Webb began to stir. He opened his eyes one morning and raised his head. 'Where are we?' he croaked to the woman.

She moved to his side and adjusted the blanket about his shoulders. 'We're in the cave you led us to. I think we are fairly safe. It has snowed again, so all our tracks are well covered. You are better and the fever has gone down.'

He lay back and grimaced. 'It's sore,' he said. 'That old bear really gave me a clawing, didn't he?'

She nodded. 'He got you real good,' she said. 'Now, you lay back and I'll fix you some broth.'

'Where did you get any meat for a broth?'

She grinned at him. 'Where else? I wasn't going to starve while a ton of bear meat spoiled. So Billy and me, we got us some bear steaks, and I'll have one for you in a jiffy.'

He laughed and Billy came to him. 'I'm glad you're getting well, Charlie,' he said. 'You had me worried there for a spell.'

Webb improved daily and, after a week, he declared he was fit to travel. 'We are about eighty miles from Denver, as I judge,' he told them. 'We can travel about eight or ten miles a day in this snow. I have a cache of provisions along the trail that we'll open and, unless something happens unplanned, we should be in Denver in about,' he squinted and judged, 'ten to fifteen days.'

The snow along the ridges where Webb led them was light, the wind having whipped it away and piled it in coulees and brakes. They traveled slowly at first, as Webb worked the soreness and stiffness out of his muscles. His back was sore and at night Sara bathed it in hot water and soaks, relaxing the torn muscles. It was during this time that Webb began to notice her, eyeing her more closely.

Sara Wilcox, he decided, was actually a pretty woman. She was tanned from her days as an Indian squaw, a slave actually, doing the bidding of the chief, White Bear. Her body was straight and, Webb realized, in the full bloom of young womanhood. Her clothing was scanty, she having left the Indian camp so quickly she was unable to include much in the way of clothing in her bundle of possessions, but she had brought along a coat of pliant deerskin, lined with some cloth the old chief had gathered during a raid of a ranch. Her hair was long, a rich auburn and she combed it and brushed it with a bone comb, wrought long ago by the hands of some ancient artist.

Her hands were strong, and Webb grew to love the feel of them kneading his back and shoulders. She will make some man a good wife, he thought and then, shockingly, the thought: she would make *me* a good woman, a wife! And suddenly he knew that once he had Billy in the hands of his uncle, he just might see if she would consider staying with him. She had spoken vaguely of going back to Indiana and looking up some family. As his mind held to the thought, deep in the night hours, he would awaken and look over at the mound of blankets that covered her body. She would make a good wife, and he was beginning to think much of her!

However, Webb was not alone in his observations. Sara was developing a growing feeling for him. As the days went by and she spent time kneading his back and shoulders, treating his wounds, thoughts began to come back to her. How wonderful it was to feel the relaxed and appreciative flesh of a man, enjoying the touch of your fingers. And she softened to the point where she looked forward to feeling his body beneath her hands, bringing back memories of another time when the body of a man was exciting to her. She began to look upon him more than as one who had appeared out of nowhere and saved her and Billy from slavery in an Indian camp. He was a warm, kind, generous person and at the moment dependent upon her care.

Late one night, when she roused and placed another

branch on the fire, she looked over at him, bundled in his blankets and suddenly yearned to crawl beneath the blankets and cuddle close to him. Back in her own blankets she lay and thought of the man near her, and the future. Did they have a future together? Or would they part finally when this particular episode of life was over? She fell asleep dwelling on the thought and dreamed of a time when she lived and loved with a huge man, whose tenderness and kindness offset any memories of past unhappiness.

FIFTEEN

Lightning Head waited as long as he could endure before beginning a search for any sign of how and which way the white woman and boy had left the village.

The village left the killing area. Enough meat and hides, hoofs and horns had been garnered from the buffalo to last them through the winter months. At the ceasing of the first light snowfall, White Bear, the chief, declared it time to return to their home village. By the time they arrived back at the hogans it would be time to cure the meat, and to gather in the last of the forest's roots and nuts, fruit of the land.

'When we are settled back into our hogans,' he told Lightning Head, 'there will then be time for you to make search for the white woman and boy. With good trackers from our village, you will be able to locate them quickly.'

But the soothsayer of the village had not foretold that there would be a deeper snowfall following the first. The day the village arrived at its former location, it began to snow again and continued for several days, laying a blanket of white over the landscape. Once again Lightning Head chafed and fumed. The captives and their rescuer would be further away and, for certain, their sign more difficult to uncover.

When finally the snow ceased, he and two close friends, who had ridden with him on raids against the white settlers, and had counted coup with him many times, left the village and began to search the area, slowly widening their range. One day Lightning Head stood on a high point, looking out with keen eyes for any sign of movement below him. His eyes turned south and east-ward and suddenly a thought struck him.

He recalled the small ranch where he had captured Billy, killing the two adults. That was only few sleeps from the town of Denver which, he had been told, was grow-ing larger by the month. Miners were flocking in to dig in the earth for the gold metal. Soft and pliable, he knew it had no worth as weapons. Furs and skins made better bargaining items. He shook his head. White eyes were strange.

His thoughts went back to the ranch and slowly he came to a conclusion. Whoever it was who had taken the woman and boy from the village, would go toward the town called Denver. And on the way they might pass close to the ranch where he had found Billy. When his two companions came in from their search, sitting around Lightning Head's fire with Bright Willow serving them a hot root tea, he aired his thought to them.

'We will be there and waiting for them to come,' he told them.

Several days from the village, one of the two braves with Lightning Head stumbled across the carcass of the huge bear killed by Charlie Webb. Carefully brushing off the snow and examining the area surrounding the frozen animal, Lightning Head reconstructed the death of the beast in his mind. Whoever it was who had spirited away the woman and boy from the village was much man, he reasoned. He knew of only one person who had fought with the mountain grizzly and lived to tell about it, which he did at nearly every council fire. Old White Bear did not miss many opportunities to retell of his experience with the fierce animal.

Here, however, was evidence that there had been another successful killing of the white grizzly. The body of the beast, still fairly intact due to the cold which kept natural deterioration down, told him how it died. Bullet wounds in the chest and head, a large wound in the side, in the soft area under the arm. These were signs of a desperate struggle. And the knife wound under the arm spoke of close encounter. And the bear was dead!

Lightning Head straightened from his examination of the bear and looked about keenly. The one who had killed the bear could not have gotten away unscathed. Undoubtedly he had been terribly wounded by the claws of the grizzly. His eyes followed the natural rise of the incline. Somewhere up there they had rested, allowed wounds to heal during the period of heavy snowfall. A cave? He called his two companions.

'We will look for a cave. Those we seek might still be there. The one who fought this giant had to have been badly mauled. Let's look carefully. We may be closer to them than we know.'

It was two days before they discovered the cave. It was late evening and one of the braves nearly fell into the cave entrance. He untangled himself from the brush Webb had laced across the hole and saw what he had discovered. His signal brought Lightning Head and the other brave.

Lightning Head entered the cave and saw immediately that it had been inhabited recently. Then the discovery of a blood-smeared bandage confirmed that those they sought had been here and the man had been clawed badly by the bear. He trembled with the urge to leave the cave and strike out quickly across country toward the white eye town called Denver, but reason quickly told him that those he pursued were well ahead of him.

'We will rest here for the night. Eat well and sleep. For when we leave here with the sun there will be no stopping until we reach the white settlement.'

Charlie Webb, Sara Wilcox and Billy Harris were hidden behind a copse of young pine growth and piñon. The woman and the boy crouched in the undergrowth, while Webb eased forward to the very edge of the woods and eyed what lay before him.

They had come to the boundary of the Harris ranch and were in the woods across the creek from the shack where the cabin onetime sat. Billy eyed the place carefully and slowly came to realize where they were.

'Hey,' he whispered excitedly to Webb. 'That's my place, that's the chimney to our cabin.'

Webb turned and put a finger to his lips. 'Shhh. Voices carry a long way. Yes, that's your place. But it looks like someone has moved in.'

'Well,' the boy protested stoutly, 'they'll jist have to move on! They cain't—'

Webb placed a broad palm over the lad's mouth. 'You have to be quiet, Billy. You and Sara hunker down here and I'll look around awhile. Just stay here 'til I get back.'

Sara tugged the boy to her and he quieted. Webb nodded and disappeared into the woods surrounding the house.

He had noticed there were six horses in the corral. It

was late afternoon, with little wind and, his knowledge of weather and the mountains told him, it was going to snow again. He wanted to get away from the ranch and whoever it was housing presently before full dark. However, it was partly curiosity that caused him to pause in their journey to find out just who might be using the ranch. Whoever it was had thrown up a rough shanty, and a shed for the animals. The corral showed fresh posts and rails. Apparently they had moved in just before winter had begun and had hurriedly erected shelter for man and beast.

He moved to a point closer to the house and settled in to watch. He counted five men, moving in and around the house and shed. The cook and the foreman or boss, he surmised, did not leave the warmth of the fireplace, up against which the shanty was placed. Darkness came and he moved around to where Sara and Billy were waiting.

'I'll be gone a while. I'm going to borrow us some hosses. If I get in trouble and you hear shooting, you head for Denver.' He pointed. 'It's that way, south and east. After three days you'll see smoke. That's the town. Billy knows where his uncle lives. That's all in case I get into trouble. Don't worry, I'll be back.' And with that he was gone into the shadows of the trees. Billy shivered.

'I know the way once we get to town, but I don't know the way from here to town.'

She hugged him close. 'Don't worry, Billy. Charlie Webb will be back and with horses.' She squeezed him tightly. 'No five men can outdo Charlie Webb. If he can whip a grizzly, he can whip a paltry five men!' Billy snuggled close to her, somewhat mollified.

Webb moved back of the shed where he could hear the horses inside, munching on hay and snuffling now and then. He awaited midnight. Also, he was not certain that those within the shack would not send a guard for the animals. He crouched and waited, hidden beneath a low-spreading pine, shielded by the build-up of snow around the tree.

It was mid-evening when a man came from the shanty to the shed, checked on the horses tethered within, and looked at those still in the corral. He apparently spread some hay, and then the unforeseen happened. He stepped around the corner of the horse shelter and relieved himself. It was then that his eyes saw Webb's tracks around the shed. He crouched and searched with his eyes into the underbrush and around the shed. He was immediately in front of Webb when he bent to look under the pine where Webb was crouched. As he did so the big man rose and a huge fist met the jaw of the searcher. The man flew back, crashing against the wall of the shed and then slid down into the snow, unconscious.

Webb quickly dragged the man into the shed, over against the side wall, away from the now uneasy horses, and tied him with a lariat that was hanging from a post. Taking the man's bandanna from about his throat, he stuffed it into the man's mouth, and with a pigging-string tied it into place. This done he rose and stepped to the shed opening. He watched the house carefully for several moments. Seeing no movement, he quietly saddled two of the horses and led them from the shed.

Keeping in the shadows of the tree-line, he appeared before Sara and Billy leading the animals. The deep snow covered the sound of their movement. He motioned to the woman and Billy.

'Sara, you ride this one, with Billy at back of you. I'll lead out and you follow. Be as quiet as possible. We've been lucky so far.'

In a moment they were mounted. Sara noticed a blanket roll back of each saddle. He's thinking, she thought with a small smile. At least we'll be warm when we take time to sleep.

It was well into the evening when Laff Brock noticed one of the men was not in the shack. 'Whar's Slim?' he asked one of the men.

The man looked around. 'He went outside a while ago to check on the hosses. Guess he ain't come back yet.'

'How long ago did he leave?'

The man shrugged. 'Hour, maybe a little longer. He may be brushin' his hoss down. He's particular about his hoss.'

Brock thought a moment and then motioned to one of the men. 'You come with me. Let's check on Slim. He's been out a good spell.'

In a few minutes they entered the shed. A grunting and thrashing about brought them to the trussed body of Slim.

Quickly they unbound him and removed the gag from his mouth.

'What happened to you?' asked Brock, scowling at the man.

Slim worked his mouth, swallowed drily and croaked. 'They was someone back of the hoss shed here. I located him in the bushes, but he busted out like a bear and next thang I knew I was roped like a calf at brandin' time.'

'Laff,' called the man with him. 'Thar's two hosses gone. Saddles an' all.'

Brock swore. 'You go roust the rest of the men out. Maybe we can trail them. Slim, you saddle up the rest of the hosses.'

A group of grouchy men came from the shack and in

a few minutes were mounted. Brock thought a moment. 'Let's spread out and see if we can find some tracks in the snow.'

As he spoke the clouds opened and once again began laying a white, cold blanket on the ground. In a few minutes all signs of any movement away from the area were covered, obliterated by the fluffy flakes drifting from the sky, covering all signs that might have led them after their unwelcome visitors.

SIXTEEN

Three men sat around a table in the Denver saloon. Clarence Harris, the owner, Hank Culpepper, the town marshal and Will Martin, the town's banker. Over cups of coffee, one or two laced pleasantly with a touch of pure Kentucky mash, they discussed the probability of trouble in the town.

'That Roman McClure may call himself a rancher,' said Hank Culpepper. 'But I've wired at least a half-dozen sheriffs near and further away, and no one knows of a herd being held for shipment in the Denver area for Roman McClure. Along with that,' he shoved the flyer he had found across the table to Will Martin. 'McClure is wanted for bank robbery in about three states. I'd say, we've got a bank hold-up brewing for you, Will. And we oughtta be prepared for it.'

'How about his foreman, Brock?' asked Clarence, wincing as he thought of the beating Brock had given him a month ago. 'I'd bet my bottom dollar he's as guilty as his boss, McClure.'

Will Martin stirred uneasily in his chair. 'There's not much we can do, fellows. Hank here can't watch my bank twenty-four hours a day.' He looked at Hank. 'Have you

118

got in touch with the sheriff of the territory? Shouldn't he be made aware of what we think might happen here?'

Hank sipped from his cup and cleared his throat. 'The sheriff has been wired about our suspicions. But I ain't heard from him yet. He's got a mighty big territory to cover.'

'Well,' Clarence leaned forward and touched up his cup with a touch of the mash, 'here's what I think we can and perhaps should do.'

Lightning Head and his two companions lay in the bushes and small growth on the tree-line before the shack which housed McClure and his men. They had been in place for several hours, since early morning, waiting for some sign of movement. They saw that there were four horses in the corral, so they knew there were at least that many men in the shack.

Lightning Head touched one of his braves on the arm and gestured with his chin. Smoke began to rise from the chimney. Slowly at first, then as the fire grew larger inside the shack, the smoke rose firmly in a column above the chimney. The three Indians watched.

One man came out, relieved himself at the corral, and counted the horses. He stretched and, turning slowly, searched the tree line, squinting in the early morning glare of the sun on the newly fallen snow. He paused only briefly and went back into the cabin.

Lightning Head motioned to the others and they retreated back into the woods. He drew them closely to him and began talking in a low voice.

'These white eyes are on our land. More and more they come. Here there are only two more than us, if there is only one man to a horse. What do we do, braves

of the Utes? Walk away and let these white eyes live to
bring in more of their brothers to occupy our land?'

'There is only one hand of fingers in the cabin,' said
one of the braves. 'If we are wise, we can kill them all and
then continue on our quest.' The other agreed.

The three crept close to the corral. There they settled
to wait for the occupants of the shack to begin their daily
routine. Slim opened the door to go attend the horses,
followed by one other. As they closed the door behind
them, Lightning Head and his braves struck!

A bow-string hummed and an arrow entered Slim's
chest, to emerge from the back, his heart and lungs
pierced by the one bolt. The man with him yelled, and
turned to dash back into the shack, when another arrow
whispered through the early morning air, and struck him
in the kidneys, penetrating through to his bowels. He
screamed in pain and fell, scrambling to climb the one
step into the shack. He died with one hand on the door.

Knowing there was only one door to the shack,
Lightning Head cocked the one rifle they had and posi-
tioned himself so he had a clear field of fire to the door.
After the man's last scream and scrambling at the door,
all was silent.

Inside, McClure and Brock shook themselves awake
and found their rifles. There were only four of them.
'Only Injuns woulda come up that quiet,' Brock
surmised. 'Them two boys are done with. We're holed up
here like pigs in a poke. They fire the shack and we have
to run out that door, we're dead ducks.'

Lightning Head chafed under the delay in his search for
the woman and the boy. He was certain, now, that they
were on their way to the white eye town of Denver, and it
was still a long way, and the snow was again deep.

He motioned to one of the braves. They talked quietly and the brave nodded and left. Minutes passed and then the brave appeared upon the shaky roof of the shack carrying a horse blanket. He wadded it up and shoved it into the chimney hole, turned and signaled to Lightning Head and disappeared from the roof.

The strategy of the Indians paid off in a few minutes. The men in the cabin withstood the gathering wood smoke as long as possible and suddenly the door of the shack burst open and three men leaped from it, coughing and wiping their eyes. As they staggered about, the brave concealed at one corner of the cabin leaped out and with his hatchet struck one of them to the ground. The others drew their sixguns and began firing at random, their eyes streaming from the acrid smoke. Before their vision cleared they were writhing in the snow, one with an arrow through his chest, and the other unconscious from a blow from the brave's hatchet as he entered the struggle. However, the tide turned quickly.

Brock and McClure eased out of the shack, staying underneath the smoke. Lying in the snow beside the cabin, they began firing with their rifles. The brave concealed beside Lightning Head rose to release another arrow, and was drilled through the chest by Brock's slug. McClure sighted in on the Indian who had taken two of his men with a hatchet and drilled him through the stomach and chest. In a few brief moments, quietness spread across the slope, echoes of the yells and gunfire dying in the distance.

Lightning Head saw his two companions fall. He had the desire to throw himself at Brock and McClure, but reason halted his anger and inclination to attack the two remaining whites. They had rifles, apparently the kind that fired many bullets in a short time. He had the one old weapon, which might fire and might not, the shell being so old. He laid the rifle aside, unfired, and slipped away into the woods. There he found a niche in the bole of a giant pine, where he could watch and listen. When night came he would retrieve the bodies of his two friends, leaving them where they could be found later by their families. It was a bitter thought that he must now report the incident to Chief White Bear, and carry a message of sorrow to the families of the two fallen braves.

After removing the bodies of his friends, Lightning Head planned his next move, which would be to find the woman and the boy. The village of Denver was not far away. It was there he would find them, he was certain. Without further thought he settled into his hiding place and awaited darkness, at which time he would retrieve the bodies.

Brock and McClure watched the day through, deciding that if any Indians remained out there, they had drifted away after losing two of their band.

'Leave them redskins where they are,' said Brock. 'We'll drag them to a nearby coulee and turn some dirt over them.'

The two men stayed in the house, drinking coffee and taking turns watching. When evening came, Brock ventured from the cabin to see if their horses had been let out of the corral. Finding the horses still there, he tossed them some hay from the shed and turned them loose to drink from the creek. Once they were back in the corral, he started for the shack, when a thought came to him. Where were the bodies of the Indians?

He and McClure had exposed themselves long enough to place the bodies of the crew against the foundation of the shack. There, covered with snow, they would remain until the weather cleared and they could be buried. The bodies were still there, intact.

The bodies of the two Indians were gone. If there were others of the Indian party, they had withdrawn. The shack was no longer under siege.

SEVENTEEN

The sun was dropping behind the high peaks of the mountains when Webb signaled for them to stop. They sat their horses at the edge of the village, now rapidly becoming a town, of Denver. The wind was cold, their faces numb with chill. Webb turned around in the saddle.

'Billy,' he said to the boy sitting behind him. 'We'll let you guide us now. Can you find your uncle's house from here?'

The boy, weary and sagging from so much riding for long hours and in the cold, straightened and looked about him. He pointed down the street they were ready to enter.

'That's my Uncle Clarence's saloon,' he said, his voice suddenly animated. 'The street this side of the saloon goes back a-ways, and his house is at the end of it.'

'Come up here, and guide us,' Webb said. He reached back and helped the boy to the ground and then removed his boot from the stirrup. Billy clambered up the side of the horse, helped by Webb's lifting him and, seated before him, pointed to the street he had mentioned. Webb gigged the horse and, with Sara beside them, they rode into the street. A cold wind was sweeping in from the mountains, and there was no one about. Two or three horses stood at the hitch rail before the saloon, their backs turned to the wind.

Clarence Harris's house was at the end of the street, backed up against what was, during the summer growing season, a large garden, fenced in with whitewashed poles and pickets. The house itself was large, smoke rising from two fireplaces. Billy pointed to the house.

'There, that's my Uncle Clarence's place. I've been here lots of times.'

They drew their mounts up to the customary hitch rail in front of the house and dismounted. Stiff and weary from their long journey in the cold mountain weather, they stretched and, looping their horses' reins about the hitch rail, they entered the yard and stepped up on the porch. Webb pushed Billy forward.

'Knock on the door, son. You be the first.'

Billy hesitated and then stepped up to the door and with a cold fist, knocked on it. He shivered, either with the cold, or nerves, at the approach of this moment so often dreamed of.

Clarence Harris opened the door and looked into the gathering darkness. Momentarily he did not discern more than three bulky shapes on the porch. 'Who's there?' he asked.

Billy raised his face and light from the room removed the shadows. 'Uncle Clarence … it's me, Billy!'

Harris dropped his eyes to the small face raised to him, his mouth dropped open in surprise.

'Billy? My Gawd, it is you!' He reached down and gathered the boy up in his arms, turning back into the room. 'Samantha, it's Billy! He's home!'

His wife came from the kitchen, her cheeks already

streaming with tears. She came up to them and threw her arms about both of them, sobbing.

Finally Clarence untangled himself from the arms of the boy and his wife and remembered the two others he had seen standing on the porch. 'Webb, come on in outta the cold. And whoever it is with you, both of you come on in.' When Sara stepped through the door after Webb, his eyes widened at the sight of the woman, dressed in Indian garb.

He grasped Webb's hand and shook it, pumping it and slapping his shoulder with the other. 'You did it! I knew you could! If anyone could it would be you. And you are both safe!'

Webb returned his greeting and then motioned to Sara, drawing her up beside him. 'Clarence, this is Sara Wilcox. She was captive along with Billy. She helped me get the boy out of the village and get him here.'

Clarence took her hand in his, looking earnestly into her face. 'You will never know how much we appreciate whatever you did for Billy. Our home is your home, as long as you wish.'

For the first time since her escape from the village, tears came to the eyes of the woman, who for years had endured the torments and pressures of captivity. She bowed her head and wept and Samantha, releasing Billy, came to her.

'There, there,' she said, 'there's no need for tears now, you are safe with us. When you've rested a few days, we'll go to my husband's mercantile and get you proper clothes. But for now, you rest, eat, sleep. Tomorrow will look a lot better to you.'

Sara leaned back in the arms of Samantha and looked her in the face through tear-dimmed eyes. 'I ... still don't speak ... good English. I've lost some of it. But, I'll try not to shame you among the women of the community.'

'Hush, now, child. You let me take care of the women of this town. You just relax and get yourself back on your feet.' She scrutinized Sara closely, face and body and nodded. 'Sara, you're a right pretty woman, and when we get you in the clothes you need, you'll have all the bachelors of Denver knocking at your door.' Sara blushed and looked down. Samantha looked at Webb.

'You look kinda strung out, too, Charlie. Guess a big supper of mashed spuds, a steak or two, some other fixin's and you'll be feeling up to snuff.' She hugged him and saw him flinch somewhat when she patted his back.

'What's the matter? You ticklish or something?'

'A bear clawed him up real bad, Aunt Samantha,' Billy chimed in. Clarence looked questioningly at Webb. The big man shrugged.

'It's a tale for later tellin',' Webb murmured. 'Right now, I need to get some vittles in me, warmed up to the bone and then we'll go over our trip here.'

'He's a brave man,' Sara said simply, her eyes warm upon the face of her rescuer. 'We would never have made it by ourselves, even if we had tried.'

'Enough of this,' said Samantha. 'You get out of them heavy coats and set by the fire, while I stir up some supper for you.'

An hour later Webb leaned back from the table and sighed with great contentment.

EIGHTEEN

Lightning Head stood on an overview, hidden from other eyes by a low, spreading pine. He was still several miles from Denver, but from where he stood he could see the beginning of the buildings, the smoke rising from countless chimneys and viewed a loaded wagon on a road not far below him, making its way toward the town.

His two companions dead, their bodies hidden beneath a creek overhang, he had piled rocks about them hoping that animals would not get to them before he and others could come and carry them back to the village for a tribal burial.

He had determined not to return until he had recaptured the woman and boy, or had left them dead in the town where he was now certain they had come. Somewhere down there, he thought, among those unsightly wooden lodges the whites built, he was certain he would find them.

He was taking his time now, working his way to the town slowly and carefully. He traveled only in early morning and in the late afternoon dusk, between the last of the daylight and darkness; there was no doubt that he would find them.

With this in mind, the Indian searched out a sheltered place between two large boulders and a coulee bank, with piled leaves and small branches; spread with his blanket, he wrapped himself in the other blanket and was reasonably warm. He was inured to the weather and his strong, healthy body could endure much more than the average brave of his age and strength. His anger at the woman and boy, the causes of his being shamed before the entire village, kept a slow burn in his mind. Nothing would be right until he was able to march into the village, herding the two white slaves before him.

Charlie Webb was befuddled. He had never in all his life actually been in love. Women came and went in his life, and he sought them out only infrequently. But suddenly, he found himself drawn to Sara Wilcox. She had endured so much and had come through without bitterness or any sign of deep hatred for those who had used her as a slave. Instead, he heard her singing one day while she washed dishes in Samantha Harris's kitchen. He stepped to a doorway and stood looking at her and his heart leaped in his throat. She was alone, Samantha was working in some other part of the house and Clarence was in the store or the saloon. Moving as though impelled against his will, he crossed the room and putting his arms about her, drew her close to him.

'Sara,' his whisper was soft and hoarse, seeming to almost stick in his throat, 'Sara ...'

Pushing gently back against him, she turned in his arms and her hands, damp from the dish towel she had put aside, slid to his shoulders. Her eyes lifted to his and were warm and moist with her feelings. 'Charlie Webb, what are you saying?'

Her cheeks slowly reddened with a blush as his lips

touched her and he kissed her tenderly. Her arms went around his shoulders and she buried her face in his beard. 'Oh, Charlie!' she murmured.

'Sara, I know you have your heart set on going back to Indiana and to your folks. But, if you go just for a while, meet them all again, and come back, I'll be waiting for you.' He rocked her gently in his arms.

At last, collecting herself at his sudden proposal, she leaned back in his arms. Her eyes searched his face. 'Charlie, I have decided not to go back. My family died down there outside Laramie. I have no brothers or sisters back there. Only uncles and aunts and cousins, all dirt poor after the war. Some fought on one side, some on the other. My father came West to get away from all that. He was crippled in the back, bad, by a mean horse. He couldn't soldier, so he came West. So, I have little or nothing to draw me back to Indiana.'

'Then, if you stay here, Sara,' he asked, his voice hoarse with his attempt to realize that she was not going away, 'maybe you could see your way to marrying me?'

She lowered her eyes modestly and then raised them to meet his, directly, honestly. 'Charlie Webb, if that is a proposal, I have to think about it.' She paused, frowning as though in deep thought. Then, 'I've thought on it. Yes, Charlie, I'll marry you!'

Their lips met again, long and tenderly, until Samantha's voice brought them apart, Sara blushing, and Charlie looking confused.

'Well, now that's what I like to see. Can I stand up with you, when the day comes?'

Sara smiled at her tearfully and, turning from Webb, hugged her. 'I wouldn't have it any other way,' she said softly.

*

One evening a knock came at the Harrises door. Clarence and Charlie Webb were seated around the fireplace in the sitting-room, smoking and talking. The two women were in the kitchen arranging in their minds just how the wedding should go, whom to invite and which minister to contact to perform the ceremony for them.

'There isn't a minister in town yet, not to live here,' Samantha told Sara. 'But a travelling preacher comes around about every two months or so. He marries up them that have wanted him, and some that go ahead and live together until he comes back.'

The knock came at the door and Samantha wiped her hands on a dish towel and stepped to the door between the two rooms. Clarence was opening the door and a man stood there, his hat in his hands.

'Y'll the saloon man?' The man was lanky, with beard that had not been touched by a razor in recent days. His eyes were bleary and Clarence knew by his looks and action that he was one given to hard drinking.

Clarence nodded. 'Yes, I'm the saloon owner.' He stepped back and opened the door further. 'Come on in out of the cold.'

The man stepped nervously into the room. He jerked his head in a quick nod to Webb and then looked at Clarence.

'Y'll are goin' to have a bank robbery here in town, afore long.'

Clarence eyed him carefully. 'How do you know this? We have only a small bank, with not too great an amount of cash held there. Who would want to risk their lives for such a small bank?'

The man shrugged. 'Don't know. All I know is that I stopped at a place a couple of days ago. It was comin' on to night and colder than an iceberg. I stopped and two

men was there, both already drinkin'. They let me in an'
I spent the night. Man, did they get soused! Sometime
during the evenin' they got to talkin' about bank robbin'
and that there was one near them they was figuring on
bustin' into.' He paused and shook his head. 'I was glad
to have the shelter fer th' evenin', but I was just as glad
when I could get away the next mornin'.'

Clarence stared at the man. 'Was this a shack of sorts?
Not a real well put-together house?'

The man nodded. 'Yeah. An' it looked sorta strange,
what with a fine well-built chimney against one end.'

Clarence nodded and glanced at Webb. 'Well, I do
thank you. How are you fixed for the night here? Can we
be of any help to you?'

The man shook his head. 'No, guess not. I got me a
room in a boardin' house after I got in town. I was told
y'all might be interested in what I had heard. Hope it was
just whiskey talkin'.'

'You did right to bring it to me,' Clarence told him.
'At least set down and have a cup of coffee with us. We're
obliged to you for the news. I'll take it to the town council first thing in the morning.'

NINETEEN

The stranger's story concerning a pending bank robbery was correct. Drunk as Laff Brock and Roman McClure might have been, they were indeed planning to rob the bank at Denver.

''The weather has broken up purty good,' Brock said to his boss. 'If we are goin' to bust that bank there in Denver, this might be a good time for it. They wouldn't expect anything with the weather still not the best.'

McClure was thoughtful, then nodded. 'We'll have to be very careful,' he said. 'With only two of us now, it'll have to be well planned and fast. In and out, and long gone before anyone knows what's really happened.'

Over the next few days they planned carefully every move they would make, McClure in the bank, and Brock guarding and holding the horses outside. The time of day took a lot of thought but they finally decided that late evening when everyone was in their homes, with their families, eating supper, at least away from the vicinity of the bank, was best.

'We won't come back here,' McClure told Brock. 'They'd be on us like a bear on a beehive. They know where we are and would track us here as quick as their hosses could get here. No, we'll take off for Wyoming territory. There might be pretty good pickings around Laramie this time of year.'

Charlie Webb and Sara were growing closer to each other with each passing day. Samantha Harris had taken Sara under her wing. From Clarence's mercantile she selected dresses for her, with all the garments attendant to a full outfit from, as Samantha said, making Sara blush, the skin out. And Sara Wilcox bloomed!

One day, dressed as Samantha directed her, she met Webb at the door as he came in for noon lunch. Five feet seven inches tall, well formed, with her hair now washed again and again, and combed until it glowed with changing colors, her face touched slightly with a light rouge, she was unusually attractive compared with what he had become used to. Dressed as a squaw, in good garments as the old Chief had supplied, she had been better dressed and more attractive than other squaws in the village. This had caused jealousy, but she had stoically withstood all slurs and remarks.

Now, dressed as a white woman again, shapely and smiling in her new clothes, she met him at the door and stepped back for him to enter, smiling and looking up at him inquisitively. He stopped in mid-stride and stared at her, his mouth dropping open.

'God,' he breathed, 'you are beautiful!'

She shut the door and laughed at him. Didn't you ever see a woman dressed for a party?'

'Are you and Samantha going to a party?'

She smiled at him and came into his arms, raising her face for a kiss. 'No, but if there was one, this would be just the right get-up for it.' He kissed her and was reaching for her again when Samantha came into the room.

'There you are, Charlie. I hate to break up such plea-suring between you two, but Clarence would like for you to meet with him and some others down at the saloon.'

Clarence Harris, Henry Culpepper, the marshal, and Will Martin, the banker, were all at the back of the saloon, seated around a table, sipping their beer and waiting for him. Clarence pushed a chair from the table and gestured to it.

'Join us, Charlie, if you will. You boys know this moun-tain of a man? He's called Charlie Webb. He has scoured these mountains about us, and others, for beaver and the likes, for a long time. He's a good man to have on your side if the going gets tough.'

They shook hands around and Webb seated himself. Clarence called across the room to Tim Holland, the bartender. 'Bring Charlie a beer, Tim. Then we'll get started on our business and be outta your hair.'

Holland shook his head. 'You ain't botherin' me none, Clarence,' he said. 'After all, you own the place.'

The men at the table laughed and after some small talk Clarence leaned back in his chair and eyed the group. 'I got some information last night that I think we ought to consider.' The others listened intently as Clarence informed them of his caller and the news he carried. The news caused Will Martin to straighten in his chair and set his beer mug on the table.

'Was the man sober when he talked to you?' he asked Clarence.

Clarence nodded. 'He wasn't drinkin'. He was telling it as he understood what he had heard. And right from the hoss's mouth, so to speak.'

'Then,' said Will, 'I guess some planning is to be done, if we mean to meet this McClure and his intent head on.'

Henry Culpepper nodded. 'I've done some thinking about this kind of problem, since we discussed it a little time ago. I suggest this is what we do.' The group became serious and spent the rest of the morning planning and then tightening their plan until it seemed, to them, to be foolproof. Charlie Webb was brought into the planning and made suggestions that were agreed upon by the others. When they broke up the meeting, they were satisfied that they could meet any challenge McClure and Brock might throw at them.

Clarence walked back to the mercantile with Webb. He seemed suddenly quiet, as though in deep thought. As they mounted the porch to enter the building, he paused and looked at the big mountain man intently.

'Charlie, I've noticed that you and Billy get along good. He likes you and I'm sure that feeling is returned, from the way you talk with him. Now, with you thinking of settling down with Sara, an' all, I wondered whether I could ask you something.'

Webb eyed him seriously. 'Why, sure, Clarence. What's on your mind?'

'Charlie, Samantha and I are kinda getting along in years. Billy needs to be with people who not only care for him, but can share with him his activities. If something should happen to me, I'd like to know that he would have someone who'd look after him until he's grown up.'

Webb stopped and looked at Clarence. 'I know what you're saying, Clarence. But you have a long time yet to enjoy Billy and watch him grow up. To answer you, yes, I would see that he was taken care of and got his schooling, and all.'

Clarence nodded. 'That's what I wanted to hear. He's a good boy, a little noisy and maybe he'll get into scrapes with kids of his own age. His months in the Indian camp, being with the kids there, did him a lot of good.'

'He'll be all right, Clarence. He's a strong boy.

The weather changed into late winter, with sunny days. Soon the snow was beginning to melt. Bare rocks and ridges appeared and one day Roman McClure decided to make his move. 'Now is as good a time as any,' he told Laff Brock. 'Let's hit that bank in Denver and be on our way to better pickings.'

TWENTY

Henry Culpepper eyed the two riders who came up to the bank. It was late in the afternoon, approaching supper-time. Men were going from their jobs to their homes, relaxing after their day's work.

One of the men entered the bank. Henry knew that Will Martin closed the bank, brought the day's proceedings up to date, before he returned to his home. One of the men remained with the horses, eyeing the streets about him. The marshal appraised the tableau and calmly strode back into the saloon. Seeing Clarence at his usual table, going over the day's proceeds, Henry motioned for him. In a few words he voiced his suspicions and Clarence nodded.

'Close up for a few minutes, Tim,' he instructed the barkeep. 'And bring your Greener and take your place like we planned. The shoe is about to drop.' Tim slipped off his apron, took the wicked-looking shotgun from beneath the counter and slipped out the back door.

'I'll go get Charlie. Henry, you wander over to the livery across from the bank. Old Sam Adams is usually working with horses around there somewhere. He'll back you with that old Sharps buffalo gun of his, if need be.'

138

*

Bill Martin looked up from where he was completing the books for the bank's daily business. The lighting was dim in the room, since he had lighted only the oil-lamp at his desk, extinguishing the reflecting lights at the side of the room. He squinted as the bulk of the intruder moved closer. He recognized him as the man came into the circle of light from his desk lamp.

'Oh, ah, Mr McClure, is it? You're here late in the day. I am just closing out the ledgers for today's business. But I have finished. What brings you in at this time?'

McClure edged up against the front of the desk. 'Only one thing, Mr Martin. I have come to make a withdrawal.'

Martin frowned. He was getting the gist of what was happening. 'A withdrawal? Ah, as I recall, you have made no deposits during the time you have been in the Denver area. We talked once, but you never returned to have further business with the bank.'

McClure smiled frostily. He drew his hand from his coat pocket, holding a gun, and pointed it at Martin's belly.

'This is my withdrawal slip. You know, a slip of my finger on this trigger and you'll have a second belly-button. Now, open your safes and bring out the cash. Just put it in the cash bag you keep on hand for movements of cash for any particular reason.' He motioned with the pistol.

'You'll be in deep trouble over this, you know.' Martin rose from his chair, pushed it aside and walked to the safe. He had just closed the safe but, kneeling, he quickly opened it.

'Now, come on back here and stand against the wall,' McClure ordered him.

Martin moved over to one side and stood watching as McClure knelt and scooped bills and coins out of the safe into a bag. As he stood there he wondered whether or not the plan made by himself, the marshal and others, was working.

He need not have worried.

Henry sauntered out of the livery stables and ambled across the street toward the bank. Laff Brock saw him coming and moved around beside the horses.

'What do you want?' he spoke gruffly to the marshal, as he approached.

'Well, I just wondered who was hitching their hosses in front of the bank when it's closed, and the livery is just over there, where the hosses are usually kept—'

'Stop right where you are! I've got these hosses where I want them an' don't need no livery for them. Now, mosey on back to wherever you come from an' get about your own business.'

'Maybe he is about his business.' Clarence Harris stepped around the corner of the bank, holding a sixgun in his hand. 'Now, I think you and the man who just went inside are up to no good. Just shuck out your iron and drop it and stand up against the wall there.'

Laff Brock did none of Clarence's bidding. He moved away from the animals and, drawing a sixgun, fired a rapid two shots one of which struck Clarence in center chest, drilling through his lungs and heart. The saloon owner staggered back and fell, life leaving him before he struck the ground.

McClure, hearing the shots, sprang across the room and slammed his pistol against Will Martin's temple. Dazed, the banker collapsed to the floor. McClure grabbed the bag of cash, eased to the front door and opening it slightly, looked out.

Henry Culpepper was coming across the street toward Brock, carrying a rifle and yelling for Brock to throw down his weapon. McClure stepped out upon the small veranda of the bank, and snapped a shot at the marshal. The marshal hit the dirt, rolled and, coming around, sighted in on McClure. He fired and rolled again, cocking his rifle at the same time.

The shots, booming and snapping from sixgun and rifle, echoed down the main street of the town. Doors opened and then slammed shut as the occupants realized a small war was being waged, and the safest place was away from the windows and flat on the floor. Bullets had a way of drilling through flimsy partitions and planks.

The marshal's shot brought McClure to his knees with a slug through the thigh. As the bank thief attempted to rise and fire again at the marshal, old Sam Adams stepped into the livery doorway and levelling his old Sharps buffalo gun, drilled McClure through the stomach. The robber screamed in pain and fury, dropping the bag of money and seizing his belly with both hands. He shuddered and fell from the veranda. His heels drummed the hardpan of the street in front of the bank, then he straightened, as he was folded in the black curtains of death.

Charlie Webb stepped around the corner of the bank, facing the street, in time to see McClure drop and roll off the veranda onto the ground. His quick glance saw Clarence Harris lying still in the street beyond the two horses tethered before the bank. As he stepped into view, Laff Brock jerked around and saw him.

The wild-eyed Brock, knowing he was in a no-win battle, whirled about and faced Webb, dropping his emptied sixgun and rapidly drawing another thrust beneath his belt across his belly. He drew hurriedly and fired, the slug missing Webb by a hairs width and his thumb eared back the hammer for another shot.

As Brock's hand flashed to his gun for the quick draw, Webb's own hand darted down to his belt and came up with his sixgun. He fired a moment after Brock's shot, as his opponent was attempting to cock his pistol for another blast. But Brock's second shot never came off.

Webb's round hit the snarling horse-holder and robber in the throat, severing the artery, causing Brock's second shot to hit nothing but the sky. The mountain man eared back his weapons for a second shot, but he lowered his weapon when he saw his opponent fall.

Seeing the marshal getting to his feet in the street, Webb holstered his iron and hurried to the side of Clarence Harris. Bending over his friend, Webb saw that Harris was dead, his eyes already glazing.

'Webb, you all right?' The marshal came up to the mountain man and stood looking down at the saloon-owner.

'Yeah, I'm all right,' Webb said softly. 'But we've a sad thing to do. Telling Samantha that Clarence has bought it.'

Will Martin staggered from the bank as Webb spoke. He took in the tableau and still weak from the blow on the head, leaned back against the door frame. His feet nudged the sack of cash and he looked down at it.

'There's something in the Good Book,' he muttered, 'about money being the root of all evil. But I think, seeing what has happened here that it should perhaps say that *greed* for riches is the root of all evil.'

No one answered him. Silence lay over the streets of Denver. Three bodies lay dead and above the town scavengers were beginning to spiral.

TWENTY-ONE

It had been a week since Clarence Harris had been killed in the fight with the bank robbers in Denver.

The town had gathered at the sad occasion of Clarence's funeral, Samantha standing weeping, with her arm about Billy's shoulder. Charlie Webb stood beside her, with Sara Wilcox, whose face was tear-streaked as she wept for her friend. Clarence had been buried with honor and in the presence of his family, friends and neighbors.

Further up on the town's cemetery hill, Laff Brock and Rome McClure had been placed in pauper's graves.

'There was nothing on them that gave any names of friends or relatives to be notified,' Henry Culpepper told Charlie. 'I'll write their names in the book I keep for such things, and if anyone ever asks about them, I can show them where the graves are.' There were no tombstones for them. A simple wooden slab was marked with a name and number, and placed at the head of the grave.

It was a saddened group that gathered in Samantha's living-room. Neighbors had gone and she was with those she now called her family. Sara busied herself cleaning up the kitchen and putting away food brought in by friends. Samantha sat in her favorite rocking chair and looked at a daguerreotype of Clarence, recently made by an itinerant photographer. The lines of her face were deep with her grief. But she softly and politely greeted and thanked her friends, whose thoughts and gifts of food were deeply appreciated.

Two more weeks had passed when she asked Charlie Webb to remain behind after breakfast. He had made it his business to visit the saloon, checking on the customers, discussing with Tim Holland, the barman, the way the business was progressing. Tim was used to Clarence's presence, the owner counting the money taken in for the day, and banking it before the evening customers began to arrive.

He also visited the mercantile and talked with the partner in the business. All this he reported to Samantha. On this morning she stopped him from making his rounds. He came to the kitchen and sat across the table from her, finishing a cup of coffee she had poured for him.

'Charlie, I have made a decision that will involve myself, you and Billy.' He looked at her with raised eyebrows.

'I am going to sell both the saloon, and Clarence's part in the mercantile. Then I intend closing up my house here and going back to Ohio to look up my folks, those that are left. I'll spend the better part of the year there and then, God willing and my health being good, I will come back here and turn this place into a boarding-house.' She looked at him. 'That brings us to Billy.'

Charlie cleared his throat and started to speak, but she raised a hand silencing him.

'Billy loves you and Sara. I can see it. His eyes light up

whenever you come into the room. You took him fishing last week, and he's still talking about the one that got away.' She smiled at him. 'You can do no wrong in the eyes of that boy.'

'Billy is one fine boy,' Charlie said. 'What do you have in mind?'

Samantha was silent a moment, her hands twisting in her apron and her eyes suddenly teary.

'I can't take Billy with me to Ohio. He'd hate it there with just old folks around. I wondered … I wondered if you and Sara might take him under your wing. You can live here while I'm gone.'

Charlie rose and refilled their coffee-cups. When he sat again he looked at Samantha, his face serious.

'I've been thinking, Samantha, what you might think about Sara and me going out to the ranch that Billy's folks started. It's empty, now that McClure's gang is all gone. We could fix it up and then take care of it until Billy is old enough to take over himself. And that will be some years yet. In a couple of seasons we could have the place with a cabin and barns, fences up again, and maybe find some of Walt Harris's cattle out there in the brush. Billy could be part of what we did to bring the place back to where it was before his folks were killed by the Indians.'

Samantha sighed and nodded. 'Then you are saying that you'll see after Billy, and make the ranch his home.' She nodded again. 'It's just what I hoped you would say. I'll have a little money left over …'

He shook his head. 'There's money. Both Brock and McClure had reward money against them. It is a good amount and what better way to spend it than to make Billy a good home? Yes, Samantha, I know Sara will love the idea. But of course, I'll get her feelings about it.'

When Sara was made aware of the planning, she was excited. 'Of course,' she said. She looked at Webb with a smile. 'We will have a ready-made family.'

'The parson will be back in Denver in a few weeks. Maybe you two would like to tie the knot while he is around.' Samantha's eyes twinkled. 'Then you'll really be a family!'

Billy was approached one evening after supper, while he and Webb worked in the stables, cleaning harness and putting down hay for the night.

He listened quietly while Charlie explained the plans for his future. He was being so quiet, Charlie asked him what he thought about living with him and Sara. Finally Billy found his voice. He looked up at Charlie with a serious expression.

'Will I have my own room? And my own pony? After all, I'm gettin' pretty growed up.'

Webb nodded seriously. 'A man ought to have a place he can call his own,' he said. 'And I reckon you're ready for your own horse. Yes, I think it could be arranged. Mind you, though, there's a lot of work involved in getting a place ready to live in. Lots of hard work.'

Billy grinned up at him. 'Charlie, for all you've told me, I reckon I'd work from daylight to dark to get it.' He nodded. 'Yep, I think, all in all, it's a real good plan.'

It was a simple wedding. It took place on a weekend, while school was not in session and the schoolhouse could be used as a church for the community. On a Sunday afternoon, with Charlie dressed for once in regular pants and shirt, with a bright red tie, Sara and he stood before the minister and took their wedding vows.

Samantha Harris stood beside Sara as the matron of honour and Henry Culpepper, with a bright bow-tie and shined boots, red-faced in a tight collar, stood as Charlie's best man. The schoolroom was crowded and the preacher's every word carried to the back of the room. When the groom said, 'I do!' Tim Holland let out a loud yell.

'There, now he's gone and done it! He's saddled and bridled … poor man!'

A week later Charlie, standing with Sara on one side and Billy on the other, waved goodbye to Samantha as she boarded the train for the East. A new chapter in their lives was opening.

Billy Harris looked forward to a summer without school, and with his hero, Charlie Webb, free to go fishing at a moment's notice. Sara knew that adjustments were ahead. She was now a wife, and a mother, so to speak, all in a few days.

Charlie Webb was already thinking of the ranch and what needed done to make it a home.

They were now a family.

TWENTY-TWO

Lightning Head stood before his chief White Bear, stoic and thin of body and face. White Bear eyed him carefully, taking in the lack of flesh, the evidence of the lack of proper food. It had been weeks since the younger Indian had eaten to a full satisfaction. The old chief shook his head.

'You have been gone a long time,' the old chief said, his eyes taking in the signs of a long winter with poor provisions. 'You have lost strength in the search for this white-eye woman. Best you forget her and let your woman fill your belly again with good food. The village has eaten well because of the buffalo you found for us. Now, you stay with the village and eat and grow strong again.'

'I found the woman,' Lightning Head said. 'I know where she is and where she will be. It is my plan to return and capture her. I may kill her where I find her, but I will not rest until she is either a slave again or is dead.'

The old chief shook his head. 'I cannot force you to forget this foolishness, but it would be best. Two braves went with you to bring back the boy and the woman. You

148

return and bring sorrow to two families with the news that their men are dead. And for what? Two white eyes that actually mean nothing to the village.' He paused and eyed Lightning Head sternly.

'It is best for you and the village to let this anger go. You say she brought shame to you. But you go and leave the care of your family to the village. That is not right. Stay here now, be a brave with others in the village, and forget this woman and boy.'

Lightning Head shook his head. 'No. I cannot. I have listened outside the hogan where this woman stays with the boy. I know their plans and I go where they will be.'

With that, he stalked from the chief's tent. It was an unwritten law that any man could do as he wished, fight with the warriors, go away on his own to stray or hunt. No one could be ordered to stay or go. That was the way it was.

Bright Willow rose from beside the fire-stones in the center of her hogan. 'I see you, husband,' she murmured. 'I have prayed that you would come back to us, safe and unharmed.'

A pot of stew burbled on the edge of the fire. He sighed and sat down on a pad of furs and looked at her.

'I found the woman and boy. I will go back and capture them and kill the one who stole them from the village. Then I will be free to stay with the village and care for my family. Until then I must do what I must do.'

She nodded, her face sorrowful. She loved her husband. She was not one to bemoan or harangue. She bowed and filled a bowl with the stew, then handed it to him. 'You are here now, my husband. Eat and be free of hunger. Our blankets are ready when you wish to rest.'

Shyly, she glanced at him and for the first time he smiled. 'You are a good wife,' he said, nodding. 'I think the blankets will be welcome and someone to share them with me even more welcome.' She giggled and turned from him.

A month after Samantha had left for Ohio, Charlie Webb had formulated his plans for the ranch. One morning, with Sara and Billy seated in the wagon seat beside him, they left Denver. The wagon was loaded with those things they would need to set up a meager home, until a cabin could be built. Food staples, clothing and other personal necessities were included in the load. The horses pulling the wagon were work animals, heavy and strong. Webb's riding gelding was led behind the wagon.

Following up their leaving by a week, would be three wagon-loads of lumber, tools, and tents. He had hired six men to work with him building the cabin and stables. Webb judged that, with them all working hard at the problem, within three months the cabin and stables, with some smaller sheds, would be finished and the men would return to Denver with the wagons and teams. From that point on everything that needed doing on the ranch would be done by himself, Sara, and what Billy could do under supervision.

Three days after leaving Denver they pulled the wagon into the yard in front of the shack thrown up by McClure and his gang. Billy leaped from the seat and stood looking up at the chimney.

'Well,' he said, 'at least the chimbly is the same.'

'We will tear down the shack,' Webb told the boy, 'and built us a real cabin. This is our home now and we are here to stay.'

During the month that followed, with Webb and six other men working, the scene changed. trees were felled and hauled up to the cabin area, trimmed and cut into lengths for the cabin walls. Two men busied themselves making shingles for the roof. Stones for the foundation of the cabin were dug from the creek and hauled to the cabin site. They were shaped and squared, and by the time the first beams were shaped and ready, the foundation stones were in place.

Everyone lived in tents brought from Denver. Webb, Sara and Billy lived in one, the workers pitched a larger tent and bunked together. A furnace was created and Sara did the cooking for the men. As Webb had said, everyone worked, each doing their part, even to Billy's making certain there were always chunks of wood for Sara's cooking-fires.

The shacks were torn down and such lumber from them as was serviceable was saved for the finishing of the inside of the stables and the cabin. By the time the first month was past, the ranch buildings were taking shape. The lone remaining chimney was to be the focal point of the new cabin. There would be two large rooms, one behind the kitchen, and two smaller rooms, one being Billy's, chosen especially by him.

One afternoon, relaxing from the grueling tasks awaiting them each day, Sara and Webb rode out onto the ranch, following cattle trails to water and graze. Billy ranged before them, proudly carrying a small carbine given him by one of the men. During the afternoon they discovered at least two dozen or more cattle with the Harris brand.

'Billy has the makings of a small herd,' Webb told Sara. 'I noticed several pregnant cows and there's at least one young bull among them. There may be more to be found among the brush and woods.'

The weeks went swiftly. By the last of summer, sometime in August, Webb calculated, having no calendar to go by, the work was finished. The cabin was ready to move into. Webb had sent a wagon, with Billy and Sara, back into Denver, and brought out a load of furniture which Samantha had indicated she wanted them to have. When the last chink was filled and the last nail driven, there was a meagerly furnished sitting-room, with a rocking-chair before the fireplace. The kitchen was complete with a small Franklin stove, shelves for storage and one of the men had built them a solid table with benches for each side.

Webb paid the workers and with Sara and Billy, stood waving goodbye as the wagons left the ranch on the way back to Denver. Their home was ready to move into.

They entered the cabin and Sara turned and put her arms about Webb. 'Our home,' she murmured. 'At last we have our own place.'

Lightning Head crouched concealed beneath the low spread of a pine. He watched Sara and Webb enter the cabin and close the door behind them. His eyes gleamed. His time for revenge was nearing. He would kill the man and boy, capture the woman, and for the second time burn the buildings. He would choose the time. It was close.

TWENTY-THREE

Webb came in from working in a tack-shed. He had stabled his gelding and a mule he had bought in Denver. Tired, he washed in a pan of water on a bench by the back door of the cabin, and dried his face and hands on a rough towel. He paused and looked about him. For some reason he was uneasy. There was a strange, electric tension in the air. A storm brewing? He wondered and shook his head. No, the day had been as clear as crystal from morning to evening. Something else. A prickle of apprehension ran up his spine.

Sara looked up from where she was working at the kitchen table. Seeing the look on his face, she asked, 'What's wrong? Are the animals all right?'

He nodded. 'Nothing that I can put a finger on. But it's so quiet. Usually there are bird sounds late, with night coming on. And there's usually a deer or two at the edge of the pasture back of the cabin. There's none this evening. Seems like something is brewing.'

She smiled at him. 'Well, call Billy for supper. Maybe a good meal under your belt will make you feel better.'

When he went to bed later in the evening, the feeling of apprehension was still there. Sara went directly to sleep after a goodnight kiss. But he lay sleepless for hours.

The sun was not yet up when Webb roused. He dressed and went outside the cabin. He stood on the veranda and stretched, his eyes searching the tree-lines about the cabin. All seemed normal. Bird sounds were beginning, a slight breeze rustled leaves in a copse of piñon beyond the tack-shed. He stepped back into the cabin and donned the knife in its leather scabbard between his shoulder blades. He shrugged it into place under his jacket, opened the back door, stepped out and approached the stables.

Lightning Head slipped around the corner of the stables and stood looking at Webb.

Webb came to a halt as the Indian appeared suddenly before him. He paused, balanced and ready. He knew this was a confrontation brought on by the Indian's pride. He eyed Lightning Head and did not speak.

'You stole a slave woman from my village. You took a little boy who was learning our ways. I have come to take them back with me, and to kill you, so you will not do such a thing again.'

Webb shook his head. 'They were white, not Indian, not slaves. You stole them or bought them as slaves from some other tribe. I merely took them back to their people. The woman is now my wife. The boy is under my care. You would be wise to leave it as it is.'

'You brought shame to me, leaving me bound as an animal for my people to find. I cannot leave until I shame and kill you before your wife and the boy. Then I will take them back to my village. But, enough talk!'

Lightning Head was carrying a war club, a heavy club with one end enlarged and bound with leather. Webb had no illusions about the item. He had seen them

wielded and knew their destructive power. In the hands
of an expert they were deadly weapons. The Indian gave
a shout, and lunged toward Webb, swinging the heavy
club before him.

As he came close, Webb dodged and as Lightning
Head swept past him, the club missing his head by mere
inches, Webb slammed his fist into the Indian's side.
Lightning Head grunted and spun about from the blow,
nearly losing his footing. He gathered himself and dived
at Webb's knees, thinking to bring him down for a better
advantage with the club.

Again Webb ducked him, but as the Indian slipped
past him, the club struck Webb's shoulder. His entire left
side went numb. He gritted his teeth at the pain and
found he could hardly move his left arm. The Indian had
seen this, and with a triumphant yell, dived for Webb, the
club poised to come down on his head.

Sara stood on the back stoop of the cabin, her eyes
wide with horror, her hands over her mouth. Billy came
rushing out of the house and, seeing Webb fighting the
Indian, raced back in and came out with his carbine.

'Get out of the way, Charlie,' he yelled. 'I'll shoot
him!'

'Don't,' Sara seized the gun-barrel and forced it down.
'You might hit Charlie. Put it down!' Billy did as she bade
him, his eyes following the action of the two men struggling. He was pale and excited. His eyes missed no movement of the struggling white man and the Indian.

Webb realized that the Indian, having immobilized his
left side, could very well overpower him at this point. As
Lightning Head darted at him, raising the war club for a
final blow, Webb reached for his knife and threw it. The
morning sun gleamed upon the bright blade as it spun
through the air.

There was a dull *thud* as the knife whirled and struck the Indian, the blade entering his chest, hilt-deep. Lightning Head grunted and hesitated in full stride, stumbling. He dropped the war club and, seizing the knife with both hands, attempted to yank it from his body. But the blade was in deep, past the sternum, the point severing the large arteries entering the heart. He coughed and raised his face, twisted in pain, surprise and hatred, and glared at Webb. Then he fell, his hand still grasping the knife. His body quivered momentarily, shivered in death throes, and then was still.

Webb staggered to the stable wall and leaned against it. His whole left side tingled, his arm and hand numbed by the vicious blow from the war club. Sara ran to him, followed by Billy, who still carried his carbine.

'Charlie … oh, Charlie! Are you hurt bad?' She put her hands on his face and looked into his eyes, her own wide with fear.

Webb reached up and touched her face with his right hand. 'He jolted me real good with his club, but I don't think anything's broken.' He sighed and straightened with a groan. 'Well, I reckon our troubles with that particular tribe are over.'

Billy was eyeing the body. 'What will we do with Lightning Head's body?'

Webb looked down at the body of the Indian who had figured so largely in Billy and Sara's life. 'I think he deserves a real burial. I'll build a coffin and we'll bury him out there, under some big tree. That is the most we can do for him.'

The weeks and months sped by. Charlie and Sara spent hours working to make their new home livable before winter came. Charlie hired an out-of-work cowboy who came through looking for work, and the two of them scoured the bushes and brakes of the land previously grazed by Walt Harris's small herd. Eventually they moved what they found to the pastures nearer the cabin and Webb realized that Billy's small herd had grown considerably.

One evening Sara came to where Charlie and Billy were clearing a small area for a garden. 'Supper's ready,' she told them. Billy ran ahead to wash up, leaving them walking slowly back to the house.

'I have been amazed how much we have done here in such a short time,' he said.

She took his hands and held them close to her. 'These hands have built us a home, Charlie,' she murmured. 'I wonder …'

'You wonder what?' he paused and put his arms about her. 'What are you wondering about?'

She lifted his hands to her lips and kissed them. 'I wonder if these hands, which have built a cabin and stables, and have done so much, are also capable of making … a cradle!'